William Theodore Bailey

Richfield Springs and Vicinity

William Theodore Bailey

Richfield Springs and Vicinity

ISBN/EAN: 9783337368760

Printed in Europe, USA, Canada, Australia, Japan

Cover: Foto ©Andreas Hilbeck / pixelio.de

More available books at **www.hansebooks.com**

RICHFIELD SPRINGS

AND VICINITY.

HISTORICAL, BIOGRAPHICAL, AND DESCRIPTIVE.

BY

W. T. BAILEY.

———————————

A. S. BARNES & COMPANY.

NEW YORK AND CHICAGO.

1874.

INTRODUCTION.

AUTHENTIC annals are always desirable. The conspicuous circumstances connected with the early settlement of any town, are no doubt interesting to those who become identified with its growth and prosperity, and especially, if by some fortuitous circumstance, unusual celebrity attaches to the particular locality.

Situated just outside the line of territory distinguished in the annals of American history, we find our only resource of information without prestige; and confined exclusively to the oral statements of aged citizens of this region. These forms are fast fading away, and with them a knowledge of many of the early events will pass into irretrievable oblivion. Deeply impressed with the great importance of securing at least a share of this information before it shall be forever too late, we have attempted, at no small sacrifice of time and labor, to collect these reminiscences, and give a brief history of Richfield Springs, its first settlement, growth, and present condition; and have noticed some of the leading features of the adjoining towns, that may prove of interest to some. We have also given short biographical sketches of a few of the leading men, who have been identified with this place and immediate vicinity; and have noticed briefly some of those now living far beyond the allotted age of man. We have been particularly careful to admit nothing into these pages but facts from the most reliable sources. The constantly growing importance of this village, annually attracts many strangers to the place during the summer months, for the use of its "*Mineral Waters*," as well as for pleasure and recreation. This consideration, in connection with the pleasure it may afford those who regard it with especial love as the place of their nativity, first induced the attempt to prepare this volume. Around the place of our birth, there is always thrown a veil of the most delightful illusion, that time can never entirely obliterate. This love is no doubt strengthened by familiarity with past events, and, as time advances, reverence and recollection add their influence to the natural affections. If in the effort to prepare this work, we shall be so fortunate as to meet the *reasonable* expectation of the people of this place and vicinity, we shall have achieved all that our ambition can crave, or our most sanguine hopes have ever anticipated.

We have also designed the work as a guide to the invalid, for the convenience of those who seek information in the use of these invaluable " waters ; " and we acknowledge especial obligation to Drs. W. B. Crain, and N. Getman of this place, for their elaborate articles on this important subject.

And our acknowledgments are also due to Mr. O. C. Brown of this place, for his assistance in the arrangement of the work.

Trusting that our labors have not been in vain, we now submit the work to the public.

W. T. B.

Richfield Springs, March 24th, 1874.

INDEX.

Richfield Springs and Vicinity.

TOPOGRAPHY.

NEAR the geographical centre of the great State of
.New York lies the wealthy and populous County of
Otsego, occupying a high elevation, and profusely diversified by romantic valleys, wood-covered mountains, rapidly
flowing streams, and placid lakes.

The face of this section of the country is generally
uneven ; its valleys run nearly north and south, in which
are Otsego and Canadarago Lakes, and through which
flow several streams, forming the eastern and western
branches of the Susquehanna River. To the north of
these valleys is an extensive plain or table-land, in which
many of the smaller streams take their rise. This is an
elevated and extremely healthful region, situated on the
dividing ridge or water-shed of the Heidelberg or limestone division, twelve hundred feet above the valley of the
Mohawk at the nearest point, and nearly two thousand
feet above tide.

On this elevated plain, in a gentle depression at the
head of Lake Canadarago, lies the young and flourishing
village of Richfield Springs, that has already attained a
popular celebrity for the numerous " Mineral Springs "

that abound within the corporate limits of the village and
immediate vicinity. This place is situated sixty-five
miles directly west from Albany, the capital of the State,
on the line of the Great-western turnpike. The location
is remarkable for natural beauty, not only in its immediate surroundings, but it occupies a position in the midst
of the most charmingly diversified mountain and lake
scenery : the mountain-sides in many instances, and
especially where bordering upon lakes or streams, are
jutted with immense ledges of rocks, or cut with deep
ravines that assist so extensively in giving that romantic
character to this portion of the State of New York,
which it so eminently possesses. Six beautiful lakes are
distributed in this vicinity almost within sight of each
other ; and this was known to be a region of popular resort
of the aboriginal tribes of the valley of the Mohawk and
western part of the State before the whites encroached
upon the original possessors of the territory. Unlike
the spasmodic growth of many Western towns, with their
restless and ever-changing population, this village has
grown gradually in size and public favor, until it now
has a population of nearly fifteen hundred, with rapidly
increasing accessions from year to year. The place has
attained an exalted popularity by the efficacy of its mineral waters in the treatment of many forms of chronic
diseases, as hundreds of cases can attest. All the appointments of a first-class watering-place can here be found.
Large and commodious hotels and many private boarding
houses having been recently erected, which will be duly
noticed in the following pages.

HISTORY.

" At the commencement of the Revolutionary War,
all that portion of the State of New York lying west of
a line running north and south nearly through the centre
of the present County of Schoharie, was known and designated as ' Tryon County,' in honor of William Tryon,
then Governor of the province." The present County
of Otsego was embraced within this territory, and was at
the time of the Revolution an almost unbroken wilderness, with the exception of a few small settlements on its
extreme eastern border, among which Cherry Valley is
noted as the scene of a most revolting Indian massacre,
in the autumn of 1778.

" John Lindesay was the first settler at Cherry Valley
in 1740, and during the first winter the snow fell to so
great a depth that it was impossible for him to go to the
nearest settlement, which was fifteen miles distant.

" His provisions gave out, and his family were in
danger of starvation. In this extremity they were visited
by an Indian, who came on snow-shoes, and who on
learning their situation undertook to supply them with
food. He went to the Mohawk and returned with a
load of provisions, and continued his visits of mercy until
the close of the winter. Mr. Lindesay afterward left the
place, and the fear of Indian hostilities prevented the
rapid growth of settlements in the county until after
the close of the Revolution." We can scarcely realize
the fact that less than a century ago, the vast extent of
territory comprising Central New York lay in its pristine
state, untrodden save by the foot of the Indian and the
trapper, who left scarce a trace of their footsteps or a
mark of their hands upon it. Here it lay from the

creation of the world till our time, its varied and mighty resources slumbering through countless ages, waiting for the stroke of the Saxon's arm to awaken them into a beauteous life, prolific with the blessings of civilization.

In the year 1755, John Tunnicliff resided in Derby, England, where he owned a large and valuable estate, with extensive forests in which were preserved a variety of game for the diversion of himself and numerous friends. Like nearly all his descendants, he was extremely fond of the sports of the chase; and on one occasion he pursued and shot a deer in the forest of an English nobleman, who prosecuted him for the offence. This circumstance, it is said, together with the onerous tax imposed by King George II. on all gamesters, so incensed him that he at once resolved to emigrate to the American colonies, where he could be at liberty to enjoy the pleasures of the forest unrestrained by stringent laws or the caprice of titled nobility.

Accordingly the following year he arrived in Philadelphia. Extensive tracts of public land had already been granted to individuals and companies by the English Colonial Government in the eastern part of the colony of New York, and Mr. Tunnicliff visited this portion of the State in search of land, with a view of making it a future home for his family. Proceeding westward from Albany, he at length reached Cherry Valley, where he learned of the existence of a region of beautiful lakes and numerous mill-streams a few miles further to the west. He was desirous of securing a location that would resemble, as far as possible in its topography, his estate in England, and, amid the unlimited diversity before him, finally selected a tract of twelve thousand acres,*

---

* The lands of this purchase extended easterly to the stream known as "Fly Creek," and the region of the headwaters of this stream are designated as the "*Twelve Thousand*" to the present day.

about two miles southwest of Canadarago * Lake, in
the patent just granted the same year to David Schuyler
and others. Here he erected a cabin and commenced
the work of clearing away the forest. Other adventurers
had already occupied claims in the vicinity, and it doubtless required no small degree of fortitude and courage to
endure the privations and dangers incident to frontier
life; and especially when we take into consideration the
peculiar exigencies of the times. The French and English
nations were at this time contending for the mastery of
the continent. The latter occupied the Atlantic slope,
while Canada was in possession of the former, who were
making vigorous efforts to control the western lakes, and
rivers south to the mouth of the Mississippi, and thus
confine the English to the Atlantic coast. The French
had vast hordes of Indian allies, who were constantly on
the alert to perpetrate acts of hostility on their foes.
Frontier settlements were frequently destroyed, and isolated cabins and unprotected families fell into the hands
of the savages, who burned their homes to the ground.

Mr. Tunnicliff had frequently been apprised of the
danger that surrounded him, and resolved to leave until
the close of the French War. His farming utensils were
buried in the forest, and he returned to his family in
England. Soon after his departure, his buildings were
burned by the Indians, and in consequence of this circumstance he remained in England several years, during
which time he sold his estate there, bestowing, according
to the English custom of primogeniture, a large portion
of his property upon his eldest son, John Jr., who had
arrived at the years of manhood, and preferred to remain
in the land of *his birth*. Mr. Tunnicliff had three sons
and two daughters. The two younger sons were at this

---

* This name was pronounced by the Indians *Can-da-ja-ra-go.*

time lads of twelve and fourteen years, and the eldest daughter was sixteen.

Mr. Tunnicliff was possessed of a large property, and occupied a high social position.

At Liverpool, he purchased a vessel fully manned, and with a considerable number of passengers on board (several families of which we shall have occasion to notice in this work) he sailed for Philadelphia, where he arrived in the summer of 1758.

A farm, previously purchased, on the banks of the Schuylkill, was now occupied by the family, where they remained until the year 1764,* when they removed to Dutchess County in the colony of New York.

Although peace had been restored the year previous, Mrs. Tunnicliff refused to accompany her husband to his lands in Schuyler's patent. Accordingly, a farm was leased for five years at Schenesborough, near Lake Champlain, where the family were located with the two sons, Joseph and William. Mr. Tunnicliff now returned to his frontier estate, and found the ruins of his cabin that had been burned by the Indians. He at once caused new buildings to be erected, also a saw-mill on the stream near by, that was kept incessantly at work, to answer the requirements of the now growing settlement. His eldest daughter remained with her father at *The Oaks*,† as it was called, from the circumstance that a large portion of the lands in the purchase were thickly covered with gigantic oak-trees. This name was subsequently given to the stream that forms the outlet of Canadarago Lake, which it still retains. At this early day, there were

* Mr. Aurelius Tunnicliff, of Richfield Springs, has in his possession at the present time, a *powder-horn*, with a variety of devices neatly graven upon it, with the name John Tunnicliff, Philadelphia, August 30, 1764.

† The "*orchard*" on this estate was the first in Otsego County.

few or no roads in this section of the country, and travelling was done mostly on horseback or on foot.

A deep and well-beaten Indian trail led from Cherry Valley to the western lakes, as they were called, passing nearly over the route of the present turnpike (a branch deflecting to Otsego Lake) to the hill one mile east of Richfield Springs, thence to the lake, and down its eastern shore to the outlet.*

It was the work of several days to travel between Lake Champlain and Lake Canadarago. The boundless and unbroken forests at this time were filled with a great variety of wild animals. The elk and deer were found in great numbers, and were so unaccustomed to the presence of man that they were easily caught. The common black bear, wolves, foxes, and beavers were also found in abundance, and the rustic dams of the latter could be seen in almost every stream. The nights were usually rendered hideous by the incessant howling of hungry wolves on the mountain-tops, the utmost precaution being at all times necessary while travelling through the dark and gloomy forest. The numerous lakes in this region were filled with a great variety of fish, and gregarious waterfowl swarmed in their waters, or flew screaming and terrified at the approach of the Indian or the hunter.

" At the time of the discovery and settlement of the valley of the Mohawk by the Europeans, it was occupied by five distinct nations or tribes of aborigines, all speaking a language radically the same, and practising similiar customs, who had united in forming a confederacy, which for durability and power was unequalled in Indian history. They were the Mohawks, Oneidas,

---

* " On the banks of the stream, forming the outlet of the lake the Indians were known to assemble annually for council."

Onondagas, Cayugas, and Senecas, called by the French Iroquois, and the Five Nations by the English." (*Campbell's Tryon County.*)

The great events of the Revolution were now impending, and a warlike spirit had already been engendered among the several tribes of the frontier by their participation in the French and Indian wars; and an appeal to their cupidity by extravagant offers of reward, soon made them willing allies of the British, who immediately incited them to the most fiendish acts of hostility against the defenceless colonists. The leader of the savages in this vicinity was Joseph Brant, who was a Mohawk of pure blood. His father was a chief of the Onondaga nation, and Joseph was the youngest of three sons. His Indian name was *"Thayendanegea,"* which signifies strength.

" Early in the spring of 1778, Brant and his warriors, with a large number of Tories, appeared at Oquaga, his headquarters the previous year. There he organized scalping parties, and sent them out upon the borders. The settlers were cut off in detail. Marauding parties fell upon isolated families like bolts from the clouds, and the blaze of dwellings upon the hills and in the valleys, nightly warned the yet secure inhabitants to be on the alert. Their dwellings were transformed into blockhouses. The women were taught the use of weapons, and stood sentinels when the men were at work. Half-grown children were educated for scouts, and taught to discern the Indian trail, and every man worked armed in his field. Such was the condition of the dwellers of Tryon County during almost the whole time of the war. The first hostile movement of Brant in this region, was the destruction of the first settlement in Springfield near the head of Otsego Lake, in the month of May, 1778.*

"Every house was burned except one, and into this the women and children were collected by the order of Brant, and kept unharmed; but the men were either killed or taken captive, and carried away by the Indians." (*Lossing*).

From an aged citizen † of Springfield, I learn that in the eastern part of the town, in 1778, there were two log-houses standing near together, and on hearing of the destruction of Cherry Valley, the occupants of these houses fled to the Mohawk, driving their cattle with them. Soon the Indians came and burnt their houses, and it was three years before these families returned. There was one house south of East Springfield, occupied by a family that fell into the hands of the savages.

An Indian seized a child by the feet and dashed its head against the door-post. There was also one house just south of Springfield centre, and a grist-mill near the head of Otsego Lake. The Indians threw the large stone from the mill, but did not burn the building.

"In the month of June (1778), Captain McKean, at the head of some volunteers, was sent to reconnoi-tre Brant's encampment at Oquaga (Broome County). McKean's headquarters were at Cherry Valley. On his way down the valley of the Charlotte River, he learned that large war-parties were out, and fearing a surprise, thought it prudent to return. He halted an hour to refresh, and wrote a letter to Brant, censuring him for his predatory warfare, and intimating that he was too

---

* I am unable to ascertain the exact location of this first settle-ment in Springfield, *thus destroyed.*—B.

† Mrs. Burnham, who has been a resident of Springfield seventy-eight years, now ninety-five years of age (1874). (*Z. E. Lay, Esq.*)

cowardly to show himself in open and honorable conflict. McKean challenged him to meet him in single combat, or with an equal number of men, to try their skill, courage, and strength, and concludes by telling him that if he would come to Cherry Valley, they would change him from a Brant to a goose. This was an injudicious movement, and doubtless incited the Sachem in some degree to join Butler, a few months later, in desolating that settlement." (*Lossing.*)

During this time, Brant's visits were frequently extended to the remotest settlements and cabins in the valleys of the Susquehanna and Canadarago, and he was well known to the Tunnicliff family at The Oaks, who treated him and his comrades on all occasions with the utmost kindness, being actuated by policy under the peculiar circumstances of the times. Being a firm adherent to the cause of Great Britain, Mr. T. refused to renounce his original allegiance to the crown.

On the occasion of the first visit of Brant to the house of Mr. Tunnicliff, and while standing near the daughter,* he twined the heavy ringlets of her hair through his brawny fingers, and remarked, "What a beautiful scalp this would make, to adorn the belt of a young warrior!" Inquiring for her father, he was directed to a distant meadow, where Mr. Tunnicliff was at work with his scythe. As he approached him, Brant inquired, "Is this Tunnicliff?" Being answered in the affirmative, he asked, "Tory or rebel?" Being assured that his affiliations were

* This beautiful daughter of Mr. Tunnicliff afterwards married Dr. Jones, of Brockville, Canada, on the north bank of the St. Lawrence River. Their son, Hon. Dunham Jones, now resides upon the original estate of his father, and has for many years held offices of distinction under the British Government. Near the close of the last century, Mr. Tunnicliff built a church near his residence (Episcopalian), but it was destroyed by fire in 1840. He died in 1800.

with the former, he appeared satisfied, and said, " Then
you are a friend of the Red Man, whose scalping-knife is
ever ready to inflict vengeance on its enemies." Thus
saying, he brandished its gleaming blade over his head,
and struck its point into the breast of Mr. Tunnicliff
with sufficient force to draw blood, remarking, with an
expression of murderous earnestness,. " If you are truly a
friend of my race, remain quietly in your cabin, and
I, as chief of the Mohawks, will protect you, and your
family, in the day of battle. Thus saying, he immediately departed, and quickly joined his war-painted
comrades, and they soon disappeared in the gloom of the
forest, in the direction of Canadarago Lake. During
the progress of the Revolution, many of the settlements
west of Albany, were either broken up altogether, or
their growth entirely suspended through fear of Indian
hostilities. When we look upon the beautiful scenery
of this region at the present day, we cannot avoid the
reflection, that all over these rugged hills and deep valleys, Indian warriors and hunters scouted for ages before
the Pale Face made his advent among them ; and the
slumbering echoes were often awakened by the loud
whoop of the Iroquois and Mohawk, who prowled
through these forests in search of wild game ; or still
later, to fall upon the defenceless settlers, and imbrue
their savage hands in innocent blood. Immediately
upon the return of peace by provincial emancipation, and
the establishment of a liberal form of government in the
States, they at once became the asylum for thousands of
Europeans, who sought homes on the shores of the New
World. Regions that had hitherto been solitary wilds
for unknown ages, were soon transformed into flourishing
towns and intelligent communities. The fertile valleys
and plains of Otsego County were now taken up by

ambitious, frugal, and industrious emigrants, who purchased lands at merely nominal prices of those who still held claims or patents obtained under colonial authority. The northern portion of Otsego County was regarded with especial favor in consequence of its beautiful lake scenery, fertile soil, diversity of timber that composed its rich forests, eligible mill-sites and water privileges, aside from the salubrity of the climate, and pure streams of running water that abound so extensively, and are so essential to our farming interests at the present day.

In the year 1774, John Tunnicliff purchased six hundred acres of land in the northern portion of Schuyler's patent, commencing near the mouth of Fish Creek,* and running northerly to the present line of Herkimer County.

The line crossed what is now Main Street in this village, near where now stands the National Hotel, and included the western half of the present corporate limits. The trees on about two hundred acres of this land were "girdled" at this time, preparatory to a permanent settlement, and the erection of mills on Fish Creek. Canadarago Lake at this time was skirted by a dense forest, and its shores were bedecked by a profusion of lacustrine plants and flowers. A howling wilderness enveloped the mountains and deep valleys in every direction; gigantic forest-trees cast their long shadows far over the waters of the lake that lay in wild seclusion in the midst of the primeval forest. This was indeed a wild and picturesque region, but possessing all the natural elements that have since contributed to its present state of material prosperity so abundantly enjoyed by us.

In 1791, William Tunnicliff, the youngest son of John Tunnicliff, built a saw-mill at Richfield Springs. The

* This stream was called by the Indians the " Ocquionis."

mill-dam that now forms " Lake Clement " was built the same year. The following year a *grist-mill* was erected on the opposite side of the creek (*east side*), which answered the purposes of the towns-people for several years, except in low water, when they had to go to great distances. Says Levi Beardsley in his Reminiscences, " There were no stores near us, and if there had been, we had nothing to pay for goods.

" Our nearest mill, while we lived at the lake near Herkimer's Creek, was Tubbs', on Oaks Creek, near Toddsville, some three miles from Cooperstown. After we went to Richfield, we sometimes went to this mill, sometimes to Walbridge's in Burlington, and sometimes to Fort Plain, the latter at least thirty miles as the road then ran." The old building in which was the first grist-mill, just eighty-one years ago, is still standing, near the present mill of Mr. John Dana in this village.

The same year that William Tunnicliff built the mills at Richfield Springs, Isaac Freeman emigrated from New Jersey, and built two mills on the premises now owned by Mr. B. A. Weatherbee, about one-half mile north of this village, in the town of *Warren*. One of the mills was built on the upper dam, on what is known as the "*trout pond*." Portions of this dam still remain.

One year previous to the date of Schuyler's patent, Konrath Mattes secured a patent of one thousand acres, lying directly east of Tunnicliff's purchase, and embraced the greater portion of our present village, as will be seen by the following communication :—

"Richfield Springs, May 1, 1873.

" W. T. BAILEY :

"*Dear Sir*—In reply to your request for a biographical sketch of my grandfather, Nathan Dow, and for such

information as may have come within my knowledge as
regards the early settlers in this region, and the original
owners of the land (the present site of the village of Richfield Springs), I have the pleasure to give you the facts
as I find them from an examination of old deeds and
papers in my possession, and from the accounts which I
have heard my grandfather from time to time give of his
early life. Nathan Dow traced his descent from the
elder of two brothers, who arrived in Boston in June, 1635.
His father settled in Windham County, Conn., where
Nathan was born. He was yet a boy of fourteen years,
when the stirring news from Lexington and Bunker Hill
sent a thrill of sorrow and rage throughout the length
and breadth of the land. The State of Connecticut
poured forth her full proportion of hardy yeomanry to
man the lines around Boston, while among the few that
remained at home, the project was conceived of surprising Ticonderoga, a fortified post on the western shore of
Lake Champlain.

"They communicated their design to Col. Ethan
Allen; and a body of men, among whom was Nathan
Dow, as yet only a boy, enrolled their names among the
Green Mountain boys, and hastened to Ticonderoga.

"More than once have I heard my grandfather quote
the words of Col. Allen as he heard them, when asked
by the commander of the fort, by whose authority he
demanded its surrender. 'In the name,' said Allen, ' of
the Great Jehovah, and Continental Congress.'

"But I do not propose to follow Nathan Dow through
the war of the Revolution. It *will* be sufficient to say
that he served with distinction, and that when peace was
declared, he returned to his home, carrying with him
many honorable scars received in this desperate struggle
for liberty and independence. After his marriage he

settled in Voluntown, Conn., and devoted his time to agriculture, until the year 1800. In the summer of this year, having paid a visit to this region, accompanied by his wife, the journey being made on horseback, he determined to make this his future residence, and in 1802 made his first purchase. He lived in his new home long enough to see a great portion of the country cleared, and a thriving village grow up on his well-cultivated farms. And when, in 1841, he was gathered to his fathers, he left behind an unsullied name, and a reputation respected for integrity, firmness, and liberality.

"In regard to the original ownership of the lands in this vicinity, I find that in 1754, letters patent were issued, as the document expresses itself, 'by his most Catholic Majesty of Great Britain and the realm, King George the Second, defender of the faith, granting unto Konrath Mattes, yeoman, a certain tract of land, situate, lying, and being in the County of Albany, Province of New York, on the south side of the Mohawk River, at a certain lake called by the Indians, Can-ja-da-ra-go.' (I would remark here, that the name belongs only to the lake, and not to the Indians.)

"This region belonged, as far as the division of the country was concerned, among the 'Iroquois,' to the Five Nations, one tribe of which, the '*Oneidas*,' ranged through this section. I might further say, that as we adopt local Indian names only because they are Indian, it would be wise, in naming our streets and public buildings, to continue the proper orthography and pronunciation. Bounding Mattes' patent on the north was Young's patent, on the west Schuyler's patent or purchase, as it was called. The present corporation is, I believe, confined to these three grants, the greater portion, however, being on Mattes' patent. A subject that may interest the operators in real estate, is the consideration then paid as the property changed hands.

"The first consideration paid by Mattes was '*one barley-corn*' for one thousand acres. This patent was divided into ten lots of one hundred acres each. It is upon lots No. 6, 7, 8, and 9, that the present village stands, with part of lot No. 1 of Schuyler's patent, and a narrow strip of Young's patent, which lies mainly in Herkimer County. In 1771, Mattes deeded to Deobald Zimmerman, for five shillings sterling, 133 acres 1 rood and 13 perches of land, being all of lot No. 8, and $\frac{1}{3}$ of lot No. 6. In the same year, Mattes for the consideration of 80 pounds sterling, deeded to Franz Freba lots No. 7 and 9, and $\frac{2}{3}$ of lot No. 6, in all 266 acres 2 roods and 28 perches of land. Franz Freba, in 1791, purchased from the heirs of Zimmerman the $\frac{1}{3}$ of lot No. 6, and lot No. 8, for 80 pounds sterling. In this deed the land is described as being in the district and County of Cooper. Thus we see that in 1791, Franz Freba owned lots No. 6, 7, 8, 9. In 1802, F. Treba sold to Nathan Dow, for $1200 (silver), 40 acres in lot No. 8, 50 acres in No. 7, and 30 acres in lot No. 6. In 1803, 8 acres in lot No. 8 for $80. In 1810, Nathan Dow bought of Walter Waterman, who had purchased from Franz Freba, 50 acres; part of this was in Young's patent, and a small part of lot No. 6. In 1817, Nathan Dow bought of George Freba (son of Franz), for $2500 (silver), 79 acres 2 roods and 17 perches, part of which is in lot No. 6. In this deed the property is described as being in the town of Richfield,* Otsego County. Thus, in 1817, we find that Nathan Dow owned 257 acres of the original sale of Mattes to Freba,

* This is the first record of the name of this township that I have been able to find. The origin of the name is unknown to the writer.

for which he had paid $4480. The original cost to Freba for 400 acres being about $800, or, in other words, the property had increased in value from $2 to $19.50 per acre in forty-six years. Without reference to the papers filed in the office of the Secretary of State in Albany, it is impossible to get the exact boundaries of these lots, but from some fixed points mentioned in the deeds, we know that the larger portion of the present village stands upon lot No. 6 of Mattes' patent.

"In connection with this matter, I shall take this opportunity to allude to one fact relating to the Sulphur Spring. Nathan Dow, at a very early day, looked forward to the time when the Spring would become a great public benefit, and he often and positively stated both in his family and to his personal friends, that when the Spring passed from his possession, he should so dispose of it that it should ever remain free and open to all. Why this arrangement failed to be consummated, I am unable to state ; nor do I wish to discuss the question of the policy of making it a free spring, but merely to say that he retained at least one old-fashioned idea that seems at the present day to be almost entirely lost, namely, that it was the duty of every man to contribute something for the public good.

" This idea led him to present to this town a *cemetery* for the benefit of the general public, and building sites, at least two, for churches. So he desired to present the Sulphur Spring to the *people*. In bringing my letter to a close, I can only regret that the information conveyed is so meagre ; but, taken in connection with facts procured from other sources, I trust it may assist you in your forthcoming history of Richfield Springs and surroundings, Very truly yours,

" L. D. Gould, M.D."

In the year 1783, John Tunnicliff, Jr., came to this country from England, and located at Albany as goldsmith, his former employment. He remained there but a few months, when he purchased a farm about one mile south of Little Lakes, in the town of Warren, which he continued to occupy until his death in 1814. His family consisted of seven sons and five daughters. Joseph Tunnicliff, of Warren, is now the only surviving son. His son, William Tunnicliff, erected a store near his father's residence, where he conducted a successful trade for many years, and died in 1836, leaving an ample fortune to his six children, some of whom are now residents of this village.

At the time of the surrender of General Burgoyne to General Gates, at Saratoga, in 1777, all the camp-furniture, together with the immense quantities of military stores of the British, fell into the hands of the victorious Americans. After the close of the war, many of these articles were sold, and John Tunnicliff, Jr., purchased a large copper camp-kettle, which is now in the possession of Mr. Horatio Tunnicliff, who owns and occupies the estate of his grandfather near Little *Lakes*.

As previously intimated, William Tunnicliff became the first permanent resident of this place in 1791, and erected a dwelling on the site now occupied by the residence of Mr. John Dana. Many of his descendants are now residents of this village. He also built a public house on the hill, where now stands the residence of Mr. Vedder Cole ; and it was kept by Israel Rawson. Cyrus Robinson kept the first store, which stood near the creek, and James S. Palmer taught the first school at Richfield Springs. The first school-house in the town of Richfield was made of logs, and stood near the present residence of Mr. William Hopkinson.

In the orchard of Mr. Hopkinson is an ancient apple-tree, that is called "The Indian Tree." It was known to the earliest settlers previous to the Revolution. Is either a spontaneous growth, or was set there by the Indians more than a century ago. It has never failed to bear fruit annually, which is said to keep sound and good for one year and more. A few rods to the north of this tree in the adjoining field is an oblong mound, supposed to be the grave of some celebrated Indian chieftain, as the Oneidas were wont to visit it annually and encamp around it, threatening vengeance on any one that should dare to molest its hidden treasure, and it remains undisturbed to this day.

The great Indian trail from the Mohawk Valley to the Canadarago led close by this mound and apple-tree. About the time that William Tunnicliff settled at Richfield Springs, Obadiah Beardsley emigrated from Rensselaer County, and located first on the western shore of the lake near Herkimer Creek, thence to the western part of the town of Richfield, about one mile northwest from Monticello.*

Judge Levi Beardsley, in his Reminiscences of Otsego, says: "I was about four years old in 1790, when my grandfather, father, and two brothers removed from Hoosick. We started with a cart and one or two wagons drawn by oxen and horses, and drove a few cattle, sheep, and hogs. Myself and a sister two years old were stowed away among the furniture, and our mother with a sick infant was left behind. We crossed the Mohawk near Fonda and went to Canajoharie, thence by the old 'Continental Road' toward Springfield. At night we stopped at the

* The first marriage in the town of Richfield, was that of Ebenezer Russell to Miss More, in 1795. This wedding took place at the house of Obadiah Beardsley, and the ceremony was performed by Judge Cooper, of Cooperstown, and father of the celebrated novelist James Fenimore Cooper.

house of Conradt Seeber. They were out of bread, and could get none at Seeber's or of his neighbors, but were compelled to make a meal of potatoes. The next day we went three miles with teams, and then left some of the wagons, as the roads were very bad. My father put a saddle on one of the horses, and on another packed a bed and bedding, on which the (servant) girl was to ride. I was placed on the horse behind my father, on a pillow tied to the saddle, with a strap under my arms buckled around his waist to prevent me from falling off, and carrying my sister before him we proceeded on our journey, the girl riding the other horse on top of bed and bedding, and a yearling colt tagging after. We proceeded to the foot of Schuyler's Lake, where we had hired the ' *Herkimer Farm*,' on which was a small clearing before the war, and two log-huts." After planting corn, Mr. Beardsley returned for his wife, who came on horseback on a man's saddle, and carried the child, Mr. B. walking beside them. During the summer they cut a road to their own land in Richfield, and put up two log-huts, a short distance apart, and covered them with poles and bark. The floors were of logs split and hewn, and the chimneys were of sticks and mud.

Mr. Beardsley was the first magistrate in this town. He was the father of the late Samuel Beardsley, a distinguished lawyer of Utica, and also of Hon. Levi Beardsley, of New York, author of " Beardsley's Reminiscences."

Their sister, the widow of the late Judge Hyde, is at present the only survivor of her father's family, and now resides with her son-in-law, Hon. A. R. Elwood, of this village.

Obadiah Beardsley died in 1841, and was buried at Richfield Springs. Four young and vigorous maples, planted by his own hands, now shade his grave in the village cemetery. The first village settlement in the town of Richfield was made at Brighton, about the commencement of the present century. In the year 1808, the Great Western turnpike was extended westward from Cherry Valley to Brighton, and between this place and Albany, a distance of sixty-eight miles, there were in 1810 seventy-two public houses or inns, and these were nightly filled by emigrants on their way west, and also by the farmers of this region, as Albany was the chief market for their wheat and other farm produce.* Brighton was at one time a flourishing village, with four stores, one grocery, and two public houses. The first post-office in town was established at this place in 1817, Jonathan Morgan postmaster. It remained at Brighton sixteen years, when it was removed to Monticello or Richfield, where it still remains. Jonathan Morgan emigrated from Colchester, Connecticut, in 1816. He was a soldier of the Revolution. He received the appointment of justice of the peace in 1818, and held the office ten years. He had three sons and three daughters. His son Nelson Morgan was elected justice of the peace in 1846, and still holds the office. When the turnpike was being opened through the forest where the village of Richfield Springs now stands, a man by the name of *House* was killed by the caving of the bank directly opposite the residence of Mr. F. Bronner, on Main Street. The site of the village at this time was covered by a dense growth of gigantic pines and hemlocks. So thickly set were the trees, says an old settler, that it was almost impossible to pass between them in some places.

Monticello, near the centre of the township, is a

* It will be remembered that this was previous to the construction of the Erie Canal, when this turnpike was the great line of emigration west from the New England States.

pleasant country village, with about three hundred inhabitants. It is situated about three miles west of the Springs, and was at one time the place of residence of the parents of Rev. E. H. Chapin, of New York. The first public house at Monticello was kept by Jacob Brewster, about 1797, and the first store was opened by Whitman Randall in 1798. The State Gazetteer says "settlements were made in this town prior to the Revolution, but they were broken up during the war. The first settlers after the war were Seth Allen, Richard and William Pray, John Beardsley, Joseph Coats, and John Kimball in 1784." Still later, John Woodbury, Selden Churchill,* and others, settled at or near Monticello. David Taft emigrated from Richmond, New Hampshire, in 1795, and settled at Monticello. He was the father of Mr. David Taft, of Ilion, and Mrs. Sally Martin, of this place.

"The first church society, Protestant Episcopal, was formed at Monticello, May 20, 1799. Rev. Daniel Nash was the pastor." The first church built at this place was accidentally burned in the month of April, 1822. The Baptist church was built in 1824, and the Episcopal in 1832. The village is surrounded by a rich agricultural district, and is a place of considerable *trade.*

For unknown ages previous to the commencement of the present century, the quiet intervale that is now occupied by our pleasant village was hidden far from the face of civilization, and known only to the sons of the forest as a resort for the use of the "Medicine Waters," that their faith applied to all the ills of their numerous tribes. At the summit of a gently rising eminence, in the midst of shrubbery, and overshadowed by the lofty and majestic branches of the fir and pine,

* Father of Dr. Churchill of Utica.

there issued forth from beneath the roots of a gigantic tree a crystal mineral fountain of life and health. About three hundred rods to the south of this fountain was a romantic and beautiful lake, silently sleeping in a quiet valley, skirted on either side by heavily wooded Alpine ranges, whose giant forest-trees were boldly reflected in the deep blue waters, that were disturbed only by the screaming waterfowl or the light canoe of the Red Man, as he glided swiftly over its silvery surface. The elk, moose, and timid deer drank from its silent waters, in the wild solitudes of the primeval *forest*. Two wood-covered islands rested within the bosom of this pictur-esque lake, one of which has since disappeared, and, as tradition says, "the last of a once powerful tribe, the Canadaragos, sank with it far beneath its dark waters."

Who can tell the number of years that have passed away since this beautiful lake was first called into being, or how many cloudless nights have the moon and stars been mirrored in its placid depths? More than three-fourths of a century has passed away since the first settlers were attracted to this locality as permanent residents. With the discovery of the mineral springs, and their prepara-tion for public use by Dr. Manley in 1820, this village dates its birth as a watering-place. The efficacy of these waters was soon found to be remarkably potent in the treatment of many forms of disease, and with every returning season from the above date, the number of visitors to the place was gradually augmented. The value of real estate slowly enhanced from year to year; and by 1830, Richfield Springs became the centre of an extensive local trade. The growth of the village, and its increasing popularity as a summer resort, will be seen in the history of the hotels and other local institutions.

EARLY SETTLERS AND REMINISCENCES
NEAR THE LAKE.

The Derthick family, consisting of the father, John Derthick, and mother, five sons, and three daughters, emigrated from the town of Colchester, Connecticut, in the spring of 1793, arriving in Richfield in June. The entire household goods of the family were transported in an ox-cart drawn by a pair of oxen and a single horse. The party arrived in the afternoon, and encamped on a slight eminence, the site of the house now owned and occupied by John Derthick, Jr., a grandson. On the following morning it was determined to begin a clearing on this spot, and to erect a log-house, which was accordingly done, and the family moved in on the fourth day from the time of arrival. This house was occupied until 1808, when the present frame house was built, and the family resided in it until 1811, when the father died, and the family dispersed, leaving John Derthick, afterwards known to many of our first inhabitants as Colonel Derthick, who resided on the farm until the spring of 1860, when he died at the age of seventy-six, leaving one son and two daughters. The farm is still in possession of the family. An incident showing the great depreciation in value of the Federal paper money of the Revolution, some three or four thousand dollars of which was brought from Connecticut by the family, is that seven hundred dollars of it was given for a pair of common flat or smoothing *irons*.

Conrad House, with his family, resided during the Revolution about one and a half miles east of the Springs, on the "great-western trail" from Albany. This trail did not pass over the ground now occupied by Richfield

Springs, but kept straight through from the two little lakes, to a place afterwards known as Federal Corners, near the Canadarago, thence deflecting from the southern trail across the lowlands at the head of the lake to Fish Creek, which it crossed, leaving the present site of the village on the north. Mr. House's cabin * stood at the junction of this trail with the turnpike afterwards built. During the Revolution, when the hostile bands of Indians were scouting the country south of the Mohawk, a party visited the cabin of House, who with his wife escaped to the woods, leaving in the hands of the savages a daughter of thirteen, who was carried off, and nothing was heard of her for several years, when she made her appearance, having escaped from the Indians, bringing with her a daughter, the fruits of a distasteful marriage with the Indian who had captured her. She had named the child *Mary* "*Manton.*" Mary had inherited the more prominent features of the Indian, straight black hair, black eyes, and high cheek-*bones.* She was well known to the first settlers, and continued to make this section her home till 1812, when she disappeared. In the summer of 1795, Freedom Chamberlin and wife, two sons and one daughter, removed from the town of Colchester, Connecticut, to Richfield, and for a time lived in a log-house which stood near the Lake House, but a short distance south of the house of John Derthick. This log-house and its little surrounding conveniences was originally built and occupied for a time by a Frenchman who had taken an Indian wife, and was one of several of his countrymen who had adopted the same course. They were supposed to have passed from the Canadas through the great intervening forests, and settled on the banks of the Canadarago, as a spot most suited to their desires, abound-

* This log-cabin stood near the present residence of *Martin Goes.*

ing with all the most valuable fur-bearing animals, which included the otter, the beaver, the stone-marten, and others previously mentioned. It was a spot but little frequented at the time by the whites, and for the hardy forester only three days journey to the city of Albany by the great Indian trail, where was found a good market for their peltries, and where could be obtained every article necessary to a life in the wilderness. Mr. Cooper, in his "Pioneers," mentions this settlement as a number of Frenchmen, who had married Indian women, and occupied a section of territory a little to the west of the Otsego Lake. They had disappeared, however, a short time before the arrival of the permanent settlers mentioned. Mr. Chamberlin and his family continued to reside in this log-house till the frame house now owned by the family of Hon. Alfred Chamberlin, a grandson (lately deceased), was erected, when the family took possession, and the cabin of the Frenchman was allowed to go to decay. Among the numbers who came to this country from the valley of the Connecticut, was an Indian, far past the meridian of life, named or was called Captain John, and his son known as Sam Brushell, but whose real name was "*The Panther*," lured to this then far-off region by rumors of a beautiful country of lakes, hills, and numerous streams teeming with fish and game of all descriptions. Their wigwam was located on the Tunnicliff lands, near the head of the lake known as "*Old Fields*," and now owned by Harvey Layton.

Indian John was an "old scalper" and friend of the British during the Revolution. His time during his residence here, was almost incessantly occupied in hunting and fishing, and the sharp click of his rifle could be heard almost daily, echoing through the mountain forests in this immediate vicinity.

His wigwam was well stored with a great variety of furs, and the game on which he principally subsisted. He was finally drowned in the *Canadarago*, by the upsetting of his bark canoe, near the island. His body was recovered, however, and buried in the little hill nearly in front of the Lake House, but afterwards removed by students of Dr. J. L. Palmer; which fact becoming suspected by the Indians living in Oneida, a large delegation made their appearance at the lake, and after a solemn smoke, prepared to open the grave of Captain John. At this moment, Mr. Freedom Chamberlin appeared on the ground and forbade any interference with the grave, as it was located on his land. He well knew that had the Indians become certain that the body had been removed, their threats toward Dr. Palmer would certainly have been carried out. It was much wondered at, at the time, that the Indians were induced to respect the authority of Mr. Chamberlin, and leave the ground undisturbed.

Captain John was an old man when he died, and always deported himself in a quiet and orderly manner for one whose early years had been associated with the most fiendish acts of savage barbarity. Immediately after his death, his son, "The Panther," returned to the valley of the Connecticut, where he remained but a few years, when he returned to the grave of his father, and built a wigwam on the Chamberlin farm, in the thicket of hemlocks and tall pines noticed as we pass from the Springs to the Lake House, on the east side, and near the road where it first enters the wood. He made frequent visits to the Connecticut, and on one of his returns brought with him a small fish, dried and entire, which he exhibited to his friends, holding it on the palm of his hand, and repeating, with an expression of good

humor upon his countenance, the familiar homily "*as
flat as a flounder.*" The fish was a flounder, a salt-
water fish, never seen in this section, and he took this
way to illustrate the comparison " as flat as a flounder,"
and at the same time to allude to his original home near
the sea.

The spot where the Panther's * cabin stood is still
pointed out, and is now in the same condition in which
he left it. A large stone used by him as a sort of anvil,
on which he beat out the black-ash splints used in making baskets and ornaments, still stands where he placed
it. The Panther was a trusty Indian, and his neighbors did not hesitate to let their children accompany
him to his cabin, where they would be treated to a dish
of capital chowder, and safely returned to their homes,
the happy possessors of nice bows and arrows.

He took the liberty to cut any timber he wanted,
no matter where it stood, or whose land it was on,
regarding it as his right, as a native of the *forest*, to
appropriate its products to his own use. He had an
idea that his property, no matter where he left it, was
safe from intruders, and it is certain no one ever med-
dled the second time with his personal effects, if he
found it out. At one time he followed a party of two,
who had taken his canoe to the Island, and immediately
proceeded to manifest his indignation by beating them
unmercifully with the paddle, and left them on the
Island to get off the best way they could. On another
occasion, Mr. Olcott Chamberlin, son of Freedom Chamberlin, took the Indian's boat to fish by torch-light.
The torch is placed in the bow of the boat, and elevated
four or five feet above the water, and sustained by an
iron jack or light-iron, which is filled with pieces of pitch

* The Panther had an Indian wife and daughter.

pine, and the fisherman stands near and facing the light, which is so strong as to reveal the smallest objects in the water at the bottom to the depth of four or five feet. Mr. C. had arranged his tackle and was sailing quietly along a short distance from land, when he was ordered by a gruff voice from the bank of the lake, " *Come, shore my boat,*" a command not immediately heeded by the fisherman. A moment after, the pine sticks were scattered in a blazing shower about his head, by a bullet from the rifle of the Indian, the report of which echoed far away over the waters of the lake. This argument was sufficient; Mr. Chamberlin immediately returned to the shore with the Indian's boat.

The Panther went on one of his accustomed visits to the Connecticut about the year 1846, since which time nothing is known of him. He was no doubt a Mohegan, one of the family of "Uncas," and in proof of this he showed the figure of the turtle tattooed upon his breast. It is well known that this region witnessed its share of the fierce encounters between the early settlers and hostile bands of savages at the time of the Revolution, as it was in direct line from the Mohawk to the Upper Susquehanna.

One of these border fights was located by the earliest settlers, on the northeast shore of Lake Canadarago. It was related that a small party of whites were journeying up the east side of the lake, and on nearing the "Indian burying-ground," * near the Lake House, suddenly became aware that a party of hostile Indians occupied the landing at that place. The whites had succeeded

---

* The elevated ridge or field nearly opposite the Lake House was filled with Indian graves at the time of the earliest settlement of this region, and had doubtless been their burying-place for centuries. Many of the graves were marked by stones until recently.

in reaching the little brook which enters the lake at the landing, when they were fired upon from the opposite bank on the north. They immediately sought cover behind the little tongue of highland that borders the creek on the south, and the day was spent in exchanging occasional shots with the savages across the bed of the stream. At nightfall the firing ceased, and the whites were only aware of the retreat of the Indians when their camp-fire was discovered directly across the lake. The Indians had travelled around the head of the lake, and had incautiously built a camp-fire, so that it was immediately discovered. At an early hour the whites hurried down the lake, on the back track to the usual crossing-place on the Oaks Creek, near where the road now crosses it, and concealed themselves in the bushes bordering the stream, rightly conjecturing that the Indians would pass down the west side of the lake, cross the creek, and attempt to surprise them in the rear. They had waited but a short time in their ambush, when the Indians made their appearance on the opposite side of the stream, and attempted to cross, but were met by a volley which killed two outright and wounded several others, when the Indians fled, carrying their wounded with them. The whites secured their guns and other arms, and buried the bodies of the two savages by caving a portion of the steep bank of the creek upon them, when they proceeded on their journey to Fort Plain on the Mohawk River.

An account of this fight was related by Thomas Van Horn,* one of the party. He was known as "long Tom Van Horn," who held a captain's commission during the Revolution, and participated in the battle of Oriskany. Immediately after the close of the war he

* Grandfather of Philip Van Horn, of this village.

settled near the headwaters of the Otsquago Creek, in the town of Stark, Herkimer County, now Van-Horn-ville. In 1813, he removed to a farm on the hill, about one mile east of Canadarago Lake, the farm recently owned by Mr. Philip Van Horn, where he died March 1st, 1844, aged ninety-eight years.

Portions of the ridges and banks near the lake bear unmistakable evidence of their occupancy by the Indians, to the present day. When the road leading from the Springs and intersecting the old road, just below the Lake House, was built, the skeletons of two Indians were found while grading for the bridge near the Lake House. The bodies were inclosed in hemlock bark, and with them were found two iron tomahawks; and when the path or gravel-walk leading from the Lake House to the shore of the lake was graded, an entire skeleton was found, with a great variety of Indian beads and other ornaments. In a cultivated field near the head of the lake, there was recently found a large quantity of flint arrow-heads, about one-fourth bushel, in a perfect state, concealed just below the surface of the ground. Also a stone pestle, once used by the Indians, to pulver-ize their corn. These are now in the possession of Mr. J. F. Getman, of this village.

On what is known as "Oak Ridge," on the west shore of the lake, one-half mile from the head, are several places where innumerable pieces of flint scales are scattered around, and flint arrow-heads entire, and others in process of forming, but broken by an unlucky blow of the manufacturer, are often picked up by the careful observer. And considerable quantities of mussel-shells, far above high-water mark, seem to indicate the location of a wigwam, and the probable use for food of these shell-fish, with which the lake abounds.

The high ground on the east side of Oaks Creek, near the bridge that now crosses it, was once an Indian "burying-ground." When the road at this point was graded, about 1810, a number of Indian skeletons were unearthed, and over their faces flat stones were found, pierced with holes corresponding with the position of the eyes; and over these holes was placed a transparent substance resembling mica, through which the dead were supposed to see their way through the mythical hunting-grounds of the spirit world.

EARLY INCIDENTS.

In the year 1778, Richard Wooleber living in a log-cabin south of Fort Herkimer in the town of German Flats, was at work in his woods on Shoemaker Hill, cutting timber, when he was discovered by a party of savages, who captured him, and immediately proceeded to inflict the most cruel tortures.

He was finally knocked down by a blow from a tomahawk, and scalped twice while insensible. Not satisfied with this, a hatchet was struck deep into his head, and he was left for dead. This occurred in the early part of the day. Not returning as usual in the afternoon, search was made for him.

Towards evening he recovered consciousness, and attempted to return to his home, but in consequence of the loss of blood from the wounds in his head, was too much exhausted to do so. Seeing his horse near by, he crawled up to him on his hands and knees, and leading him to the stump of a tree, attempted to get on his back, but was too weak to accomplish this, and was about resigning himself to his fate, when he was discovered by his friends and taken to his cabin.* He subsequently removed to the town of Columbia, where he lived many years after this occurrence, but the wound in his head never entirely healed, and was ultimately the cause of his death.

Mr. George Lighthall occupied a cabin a short distance to the south of where Mr. Wooleber afterwards lived, in South Columbia. He was out in the woods about sundown in the latter part of October, 1779, looking for his cows, when he discovered a large party of Indians approaching but a short distance away. He at once fled, closely pursued by the savages, with yells of exultation as they momentarily gained on their supposed victim, who plunged into the hollow of a prostrate pine-tree, unseen by his bloodthirsty followers. He had with him a little black dog, who seemed to fully realize their imminent danger, as he crept close beside his·master, trembling with fear. Mr. Lighthall now feared the dog would reveal their hiding-place by barking, should the Indians approach them, and immediately took out his pocket-knife for the purpose of cutting his throat, when he heard the tread of the Indians' feet on the log over his head. He therefore desisted, but held the mouth of the dog firmly in his hands for a few moments, as he listened to the receding footsteps of his enemies, when all was again silent. Although his pursuers had passed entirely away in the direction of the Mohawk, he remained in his place of concealment until nearly midnight, when he ventured out, trembling lest they might be still watching for his appearance. He succeeded, however, in reaching his home in safety. This circumstance took place on the border of the south side of the Wooleber *swamp*.

* It is said that when first seen by his friends, he was sitting on the stump, and so much disfigured by his blood and wounds, that he was not at first recognized. (*J. Skinner*.)

Abraham Lighthall lived in a cabin a few rods to the south of his brother George, on the east bank of Mink Creek, near where the railroad now crosses that stream, and near the "*Indian apple-tree.*" When the war of the Revolution broke out, he enlisted as a private soldier, and served through the entire war, participating in many battles, escaping with but two wounds.

He was in that division of the army under Washington that passed the severe winter of 1778 at Valley Forge, and endured the most intense sufferings. Of the trials of Valley Forge, Mr. Headley says: "What thoughts and emotions are awakened at the mention of that name. Sympathy and admiration, pity and love, tears and smiles chase each other in rapid succession as one in imagination goes over the history of that wintry encampment. Never before was there such an exhibition of the triumph of patriotism over neglect and want; of principle over physical sufferings; of virtue over the pangs of starvation.

"Those tattered, half-clad and barefoot soldiers, wan with want, taking their slow march for the wintry forest, leaving their bloody testimonials on every foot of the frozen ground they traversed, furnish one of the sublimest scenes in history." On one occasion, as Mr. Lighthall was returning home from the lake with his dog and gun, upon arriving at a spring in the forest,* he discovered a huge black bear, apparently clinging to the trunk of a large tree, but entirely motionless. Supposing the monster to be watching his movements with no very good design, Mr. Lighthall took deliberate aim and fired; but Bruin did not condescend to move or change his position in the least. Mr. Lighthall now advanced and

* This spring can now be seen near the residence of Mr. Allson Orendorf.

fired again with the same result. Upon approaching still nearer, he discovered that the bear was dead. It appears that a small sapling that stood near the large tree, had been cut off about ten feet from the ground while bent over, and springing back to its original position, had impaled the animal by penetrating his body, in his rapid descent from the tree, causing, no doubt, an extremely painful death. Mr. Lighthall had two daughters, who married and removed to the Western States. He continued to reside near this village until the 31st of December, 1831, when he died at the age of ninety-six, and was buried near the old Methodist chapel in Warren, where his grave can now be seen.

On one occasion, while Mrs. Abraham Lighthall was sitting alone in her house, her attention was attracted to the back yard by an unusual noise, when upon opening the door she saw a large black bear leap from a small enclosure, with a pig in his affectionate embrace, and was devouring the porker notwithstanding his persistent musical resistance.

Without a moment's hesitation, Mrs. Lighthall seized a sharp axe that happened to be at hand, and approaching his majesty from the rear, dealt him a severe blow in the head with the sharp edge of the weapon, killing him almost instantly; a feat that few ladies at the present day would venture to attempt.

When Mrs. Lighthall was one hundred and six years old (in 1836), she left this town in company with her son-in-law, to spend the remainder of her days with her daughter in the State of Michigan. When on board the steamboat at Buffalo, the captain, in consideration of her extreme old age, presented her with a free passage across Lake Erie; and for the amusement of the passengers, she danced on the deck of the vessel to the

music of a violin in possession of one of the party.
During a visit to Michigan in 1839, John W. Tunnicliff,
of this place, an old friend and former neighbor, called
on Mrs. Lighthall, now one hundred and nine, and in
course of conversation, asked if she did not think of a
second marriage? With an expression of the most
artless earnestness, she replied, " Well, I have given the
subject some serious consideration ; but the fact is, Mr.
Tunnicliff, I cannot bear the idea of raising another
family of children." Mrs. Lighthall lived until 1840,
and died at the age of one hundred and ten years.

Captain Henry Eckler,* late of Warren, Herkimer
County, was out with a friend in the summer of 1781, in
the vicinity of Fort Herkimer, and unexpectedly fell in
with Brant and a party of his warriors.

The chief, who was well acquainted with Captain
Eckler, addressed him by name, and asked him if he
would surrender himself his prisoner. " Not by a d—d
sight, as long as I have legs to run ! " and suiting the
action to the word, he turned and fled at the top of his
speed, and his companion with him. The surprise took
place near a piece of woods, into which the fugitives ran,
pursued by a band of yelling savages. Eckler had proceeded but a little distance in the woods, when he found
it would be impossible for him to run far with the speed
requisite for his escape by flight ; and passing over a
knoll which hid him from the observation of his pursuers, he entered, head first, a cavity at the root of a wind-
fallen tree. He found its depth insufficient, however, to
conceal his whole person, and like a young ostrich or
partridge, that, with its head concealed, feels secure, if it

* Mr. Eckler received a captain's commission from the Provincial
Congress, and this commission is now in the possession of Mr. John
Eckler, of *Warren.* It *is dated May* 18*th*, 1776.

remains still, he resolved to keep silence and trust to Providence for the issue. The party pursuing soon arrived upon the knoll, and halted almost over him to catch another glimpse of his retiring form. But they looked in vain; and while they stood there, and he heard their conversation, he expected every moment would be his last; as he was sure, if his foes looked down, they could not fail to see at least one-half of his person. He thought, as he afterwards told his friends, that had Brant, who also came upon the bank above him while he was thus concealed, but listened, he must have heard his heart beat, as it felt in his breast like the thumping of a hammer. Supposing Eckler had fled in an opposite direction, his pursuers overlooked his place of conceal-ment, and expressing to each other their surprise at his sudden exit, and declaring that a spirit had helped him escape, they withdrew, when he backed out of his hiding-place, and regained his home in safety.

"His comrade also effected his escape uninjured, although he had a long and strong race for his liberty." (*Border Wars of New York*.)

In the above adventure, Captain Eckler, in making his escape, plunged through a hedge of prickly-thorn trees, and the Indians, being nearly naked, feared to fol-low in the track of the fugitive. This circumstance proved of great advantage to Eckler by increasing the distance between him and his bloodthirsty followers.

Captain Eckler's brother Jacob was taken prisoner by Brant and held in captivity six years; also two of his children, but they finally made their escape to Fort Plain.

Brant and Captain Eckler were school-mates, and frequently wrestled together; but it is said Eckler always beat, being a man of great strength and agility.

Captain Eckler * died March 3d, 1820, aged eighty years and eight months, and was buried near Van-Horns-ville. Was grandfather of John and Thomas *Eckler*, of Warren.

RICHFIELD HOTEL.†

As previously noticed, the first public house in this place was built on the hill to the west of Ocquionis Creek, as a tavern, several years before·the turnpike was constructed.

In the year 1810, the lot, containing one acre (on which stands the Richfield Hotel), was owned by a Mr. Graves, a blacksmith, who sold it to Nathan Dow, who erected the Richfield Hotel in 1816, and presented it to his son-in-law Robert Benedict, who kept it as a *public house* about twenty years, when he sold it to Mr. Jesse Burgess.

Mr. Benedict now purchased the house and lot adjoining on the west (the house recently burned), of a Mr. Jaques, where he continued to reside until the year 1850, when he removed to Chester, near Philadelphia, and died Nov. 15, 1855, aged seventy-nine years.‡ The regular succession of proprietors of the Richfield Hotel, was as follows, after Mr. Burgess : William H. Lewis, John Culbert, Moses Jaques, Moses Wheeler, Charles Davy, Clark Huestis, Sandusky Keller. The last named is the present proprietor.

* Christina, wife of Captain Eckler, died January 21st, 1841, aged ninety-four years and three months.

† The Richfield Hotel received the first visitors to these Springs in the year 1821. About twenty-five remained here during this season.

‡ Mr. Benedict left two sons and two daughters. The late Dr. Benedict, of Jackson, Florida, was a son of Robert Benedict ; James, the only surviving son, is now a resident of Philadelphia.

HORACE MANLEY, M.D.

THOMAS MANLEY, father of Dr. Manley, says Benton, "was a native of Dorset, Bennington County, Vermont. He came into the town of Norway, Herkimer County, New York, in the spring of 1789, opened a small clearing and erected his log-cabin, and brought his family into the town the next year, 1790. Mr. Manley being among the first settlers on the northern part of the royal grant, and a man of energy and force of character, was a prominent man in his town. He held the office of supervisor fifteen years, and was twice commissioned by Governor John Jay superintendent of highways in the County of Herkimer. One of his sons, Dr. Manley, of Richfield, Otsego County, told me his father, the first year he came on the grant, put up a bark-hut as a sleeping-place for himself and his hired man, and a store-room for such few things as they had, requiring protection from the weather. They used a blanket to cover the entrance of their primitive lodge. The needful cooking was done at the fire outside. As they were then quite destitute of such substantials in the way of food as beef, pork, mutton, and lamb, the forest was resorted to, to supply deficiencies, and the white rabbits, being numerous, were taken whenever occasion required. Not having the fear of cholera before their eyes, and being intent in felling the forest and opening their clearing for a small crop, they did not stop to inquire into the origin and causes of diseases, but threw their culinary offal down near the door of the hut, where a considerable quantity of rabbit bones had of course been accumulating.

"Mr. Manley and his companion were one night disturbed by an unusual noise outside, but near their hut:

listening a moment, they concluded, from the cracking of the rabbit bones, that some strong-mouthed native of the forest was making a night meal of them. Manley took his gun, and moving the blanket door gently aside, fired in the direction of the heap of rabbit bones; a terrific growl was the only response, except the echo of the discharge in the surrounding dense forest. The night was dark, and having struck up a light with steel and flint, and recharging their guns, they cautiously examined the ground about the hut, and found nothing except some traces of blood.

"The animal, although wounded, was not disabled from making its escape. Early the next morning, Mr. Manley and his companion took the blood-trail into the forest, and in about an hour found a good-sized bear, weary and faint from the effects of his late night feast, and the unkind treatment he had received. The bear was killed, in the hope that the meat would give the captors a savory change in animal food. But it was poor, and the meat coarse, dark, and tough. Mr. Manley was an agriculturist, and highly respected in his town and county. He was elected a member of the Assembly in this State in 1799, in 1809, and in 1820. He died in Norway, where he lived sixty-three years, on the 21st of January, 1852, aged eighty-eight years and six months." Horace Manley was born in the town of Norway, Herkimer County, New York, March 28th, 1791. Followed the ordinary employments of his father's farm, and attending school until the age of nineteen, when he commenced the study of medicine in the office of Dr. Ayers, of East Canada Creek, town of Manheim, which he continued for several years, and finally graduated at Fairfield Medical College, in the winter of 1814–15.

In the spring of 1814, he was drafted to serve in the army at Sacketts Harbor, but was relieved from this duty by a substitute employed by his father. But the doctor says, "I was willing, yes, anxious to go, for, like nearly every other young man in the country, I had learned to hate the British. For many of those who had participated in the protracted struggle for our national independence still survived, whose oral testimony, in conjunction with the history of the Revolution, had engendered in every youthful breast a most intense animosity, and we only sought an opportunity to avenge the cruelties that had been perpetrated upon our friends and nation." By permission of his father, he was allowed to go to Sacketts Harbor with a load of farm produce, and while there, volunteered as a private, but was at once promoted to a brevet commission of surgeon's mate in the 40th Regiment New York State Militia, commanded by Colonel Mathew Myers. He served two months in this capacity, or until the close of the war.

There were at this time seven thousand militia ordered to Sacketts Harbor by Governor Tompkins.

The doctor says, "I counted eighteen men-of-war vessels lying in Sacketts Harbor; the largest was the 'Superior,' with five hundred men on board, etc., etc."

In the year 1816, Dr. Manley located at Monticello, in the town of Richfield, for the practice of medicine and surgery. Here he devoted himself to his profession, with characteristic zeal and assiduity, and in a few months found himself enjoying the rich reward of an extended and lucrative business. In 1820 he bought an acre of land embracing what is now "The Manley Spring," on the grounds of the Spring House, for which he paid $75, and erected a dwelling-house for his family. He proceeded at once to prepare the spring for public use.

At this time the only place for the accommodation of visitors was the Richfield Hotel,* where but few guests could be received. Directly over the spring stood a large pine-tree, from beneath which the water issued profusely, covering the ground for some distance around with a thick white coating of tufaceous deposit. The tree and earth were removed to the depth of five feet, when the water was found to issue from the deep crevice of a large flat rock, that now forms its bed. On this rock was found the body of a large tree, still sound and perfect; also the antler of an elk, with its points ground off. The doctor thinks it had been used by the Indians for a war-club. It was presented to Professor Mitchel, of Columbia College, New York. He also found ripe red plums, and fresh-looking green leaves, that soon turned black and fell to pieces on exposure to the air.† The writer asked the doctor how long he thought these plums and leaves had been there; he answered, "Thousands of years, no doubt," as five feet of earth and decomposed vegetation had accumulated over them without human agency. This Sulphur Spring now began to attract public attention, but the duties of his profession requiring his entire attention, the doctor sold the property, including the spring, to a Mr. Chase, and purchased the land now occupied by him, a short distance to the east of the spring, on the south side of Main Street, where he resides in the enjoyment of a well-earned competence. Dr. Manley has three sons and four daughters, now living.

A laughable incident occurred while the doctor was

---

* This house was kept by Robert Benedict, the regular price of board being $1.25 per week.

† Mr. George Bell, of Jordonville, has in his possession at the present time, a "deer's horn," taken from this Sulphur Spring by Moses Freeman, about the time the spring was first discovered.

engaged in excavating the spring. His workmen had suspended a white handkerchief to a pole by the roadside to indicate the location of the spring in the forest. A countryman on horseback, approaching from the west, seeing this supposed signal of small-pox, attempted to pass the designated point, by galloping his horse at full speed, at the same time holding his nose and mouth firmly with one hand; but when directly opposite the spring, he involuntarily caught a breath of air, that was strongly impregnated with the fumes of the sulphur water. Suddenly checking his horse, he exclaimed, with an expression of the deepest despair, "O God, I've catched it."

RICHFIELD MINERAL WATERS.

MINERAL waters are known to have been in use as remedial agents among the ancient nations of the East. According to history, the Greeks were familiar with the medical properties of mineral waters, and are supposed to be the first to use them in the treatment of the same diseases for which they are used at the present day.

The name of Hippocrates is associated with the use of medicinal waters in Greece. Pliny, the historian, speaks of their use as remedial agents in ancient Italy. A great variety of mineral springs are known to abound in many of the United States and Territories, but the State of New York ranks first in this respect; Virginia next.

New York is indeed remarkable for its great variety of mineral waters, and also metallic mineral deposits distributed throughout nearly every portion of the State. Our present knowledge of its geology, which is intensely interesting, is derived principally from the surveys made under State authority, from 1826 to 1843, and from the investigations of eminent geologists, who have examined particular localities.

In some sections of the limestone regions of the State, mineral springs are found of sulphurous character, especially, many of which have attained great notoriety for their medicinal properties. Sulphur and Chalybeate are the most common, and are now regarded of great value in the treatment of various diseases.

Among the most distinguished of these springs are those of Richfield, Otsego County, Sharon, Schoharie County, and Avon, Livingston County. We propose to notice especially the mineral springs of Richfield, that have already attained a popular celebrity in their use as medical agents.

Seventeen distinct mineral springs are now known in this place and immediate vicinity, most of them containing sulphur, but varying to some extent in their constituent elements. Two of these springs only have been analyzed, viz. the Manley Spring,* on the grounds of the Spring House, and the American Spring, in the basement of the American Hotel, and are known to be the strongest sulphur waters on the American continent. The following is an analysis of these waters by Prof. Reid.

---

* First prepared for public use in 1820, by Dr. Horace Manley. During the French War, while the English army were stationed at Albany, a party of sappers and miners were directed to this place by an Indian guide, and a large excavation was made about ten feet to the east of this spring, in their search for deposits of sulphur for the manufacture of gunpowder. Traces of this excavation were visible until quite recently.

Bi-carbonate magnesia................... per gallon,	20 grains	
Bi-carbonate lime........................ "	10	"
Chloride sodium and magnesia............ "	15	"
Sulphate magnesia....................... "	30	"
Hydro-sulphate magnesia and lime........ "	2	"
Sulphate of lime........................ "	20	"
Solid matter............................ "	152.5	"
Sulphurated hydrogen gas............... "	20.6 inches	

A Chalybeate Spring was recently discovered on the west bank of Ocquionis, or Fish Creek, near the railroad crossing, which, from chemical tests, is supposed to be exceedingly rich in carbonate of *iron*, and is regarded as a valuable accession to the mineral waters of this place. This spring, together with a number of acres of valuable land around it, is the private property of James K. Weldon, Esq., of Binghamton, New York.

In the town of Springfield, in this county, are several sulphur springs of good quality, but their location will doubtless prevent them from being appropriated to public use to any extent. Also, near Cherry Valley, I understand there is a very fine sulphur spring. It is located at what is known as Judd's Falls, near the line of the Albany and Cherry Valley Railroad. The very favorable location of this spring will no doubt soon make it a place of popular resort for invalids, being a most favorable location for purity of mountain air, and overlooking the great valley of the Mohawk.

No inquiry can be more interesting to the medical profession, than an investigation and accurate knowledge of the virtues and medicinal properties of the medicated waters of our State, in their application to the treatment of disease. This subject has already occupied the earnest attention of physicians, and been studied with varying degrees of interest and success, according to the estimation of its importance. Although this may have been temporarily delayed by the prevailing doctrines and theories of disease, more particularly of the determinate and specific power of certain remedies to control or arrest its progress, the experience of distinguished men has steadily and with increasing authority established a belief in the great importance of a knowledge of the nature and influence of these agencies, and justified a confidence in the correctness of the observations by which it has been established.

It is now an admitted truth, that many diseases are cured by natural processes, and that the value of all remedies, and of all modes of treatment depend upon their power to aid and promote such processes. Rational and physiological remedies alone can harmonize with, and be founded upon the present advanced knowledge of the laws of life. We will not attempt to describe the various cachectic states of many who live in populous towns and cities with deranged and feeble action of the nervous system, defective secretion—and excretion—with consequent dyspepsia, and congestion of internal organs, conditions which, without change in external circumstances, resist, and gradually become unmanageable by ordinary medical treatment.

The special character of these waters, and also the climate of this region has been much overlooked, and had far too little credit for their positive influence in the cure of the diseases so generally mitigated and cured here. It is a difficult matter to accurately estimate the relative value of the climate and mineral waters of Richfield. But the experience of our resident physicians and members of the medical profession who have annually visited this place for many years, may be regarded as sufficient authority for my observations in this connection. The distinctive peculiarity of these waters, is their property of acting generally on the whole glandular system, exciting to increased and healthy action. To the production of this result, their mixed composition of sulphides and chlorides especially adapts and renders them most efficacious. When, in addition to their internal use, they are also applied externally, and the skin excited to increased action, their conjoined external and internal use supplies a most decisive and effective mode of eliminative treatment, and a healthy supply of purely elaborated blood thus produced.

The copious diaphoresis which the warm bath establishes, opens in itself a main channel for the immediate expulsion of properties injurious to health, made manifest by their peculiar odor. A similar effect, though perhaps in a less degree, may be effected by drinking the water, a common, indeed, universal practice of all classes who annually resort to these springs. The impression produced by the warm bath is indeed powerful, arousing into action sluggish and torpid secretions. The languid circulation is thus purified of morbific matters, and thereby renewed vigor and healthful action are given to the absorbents, lymphatics, and secretory apparatus, a combined effect which no medicine is capable of accomplishing. The carbonates of alkalies present in these waters, as demonstrated by experiment and analysis, cannot be without their therapeutic effect upon the system. The large quantity of free carbonic gas which the water contains, and which continually rises in volumes at the fountains of these springs, has an invigorating effect. Maintaining a uniform temperature of forty-eight degrees throughout the entire year, the waters are eagerly sought as a beverage by the healthful as well as the debilitated, during the sultry months of summer.

About one-half mile to the north of this village, on the

premises of B. A. Weatherbee, are several valuable
springs; some of them being so strongly impregnated
with minerals, that they are suitable only for external
use. A few rods to the west of these, and near the bank
of the mill-stream, is a copious fountain of white sulphur
water, regarded by good judges as identical with the
White Sulphur Springs of Virginia. This spring has
been tubed and otherwise prepared for public use, through
the enterprising generosity of Mr. Weatherbee.

In the treatment of chronic diseases and long-contin-
ued derangement and debility, the climate and resources
of Richfield are considered invaluable. It is well known
that in the treatment of chronic diseases, remedies, char-
acterized as alteratives, are usually employed.

Experiment has abundantly proved that these waters
are strictly alterative remedies—varying, it is true, in
their effects, according to the peculiarities of subjects,
and at the same time shielding the patient from the dan-
gerous effects incident to the use of mercurial alteratives. Regarded in this light, it will readily be seen how
wide the range of their application and uses must be in
the treatment of disease; especially in cutaneous affections, for which their high reputation is now established.
As remedial agents, mineral waters are very liable to
abuse, as they, no doubt, in many instances are taken
without advice or direction. According to my own
observation there seems to be in many instances a spirit
of rivalry between individuals as to who shall quaff the
greatest amount of the water, without regard to the evil
consequences that may possibly ensue. With persons in
health it is regarded as harmless, but "too much of a
good thing is sometimes worse than none," and no other
medicines are taken in this indiscreet way. It must be
apparent to all, that the use of "Mineral Waters," for

disease, should in all cases be accompanied with specific directions from a physician, whose knowledge and experience in their use has abundantly qualified him to give advice. Resident physicians of watering-places are undoubtedly the most competent ones to consult in matters of this grave character.

The observation and practice of eminent members of the medical profession, have demonstrated that cutaneous eruptions are intimately connected with dyspepsia, bilious derangements, gout, rheumatism, scrofula, etc. And the testimony of thousands prove that the above diseases have been successfully treated by the use of these waters.

And that this reputation is thoroughly established in the public mind, and fully appreciated, is evidenced by the constantly increasing number of invalids who annually visit this healthful and attractive resort.

"THE SPRING HOUSE."

In the year 1823, Samuel Chase, of Cooperstown, in company with Mr. Theodore Page, erected a hotel on the corner of Main and Church Streets, that is now known as the "Spring House." The original structure was 40 feet long, 30 feet wide, and two stories in height.

This house was occupied by Mr. Page, and the two gentlemen co-operated in entertaining summer visitors three years, when Mr. Page disposed of his share of the property to Mr. Chase, who immediately leased the house to C. M. Paul for the term of five years, at $500 per year. During the five years, Mr. Chase was elected a member of Congress from this county, and was in office during two terms.

At the close of the last session, his health gave way, and he returned to this place, again assuming control of the hotel, which continued for about five years.

Mr. Chase died in 1835, and the house was conducted by his widow for four years; when she sold the property to General Whitney, who presented it to his son Joshua Whitney, now of Binghamton, N. Y. He commenced the proprietorship of the Spring House under the most favorable auspices, possessing the adventitious aids of fortune, and other invincible prestiges. Being a gentleman of culture and refinement, he was well calculated to cater to the wants of the numerous guests who annually visited his house, which was soon found too limited to receive the constantly increasing numbers that applied for accommodations. The building was now put under thorough repairs, and its limits were extended. After he had enlarged, or made additions to it at various intervals, it would accommodate about sixty guests. He also erected a small bathing-house for the use of invalids, that proved a lucrative investment.

Successfully conducting this house for twenty years, he sold the entire property to Messrs. P. Van Horn and John Backus.

These gentlemen immediately erected extensive additions to the house, and also erected two large bathing-houses, 24 by 80 feet respectively. The water was heated by a large steam-engine. At the close of the first season, Mr. Backus bought his partner's interest in the property, and the following year sold the house to Messrs. Bryan and Ransom.* They made extensive additions to the hotel, and it can now easily accommodate four hundred and fifty guests. They also added largely to the grounds of the house, now comprising about five acres,

* Norman K. Ransom; died March 13th, 1872, aged forty-five years.

laid out in gravel-walks and grass-plots, beautifully shaded by young and thrifty ornamental trees.

It is now a pleasant and inviting home for the invalid and pleasure-seeker.

The "Spring House" possesses the considerable advantage of including within its grounds the popular fountain, known as the "*Manley Spring*."

THE AMERICAN HOTEL.

This popular house was first erected in 1830, by Mr. C. M. Paul, who kept it as a public house and for the entertainment of summer visitors, until 1839, when the hotel and lands adjoining were purchased by General William P. Johnson.

In the month of December, 1850, this hotel was entirely destroyed by fire. The following year the present structure was erected, and subsequently enlarged, until it now easily accommodates four hundred and fifty guests. In the year 1865, a rich and copious sulphur spring was discovered in the basement of this hotel, which upon analysis was found to be identical with its older compeer of the Spring House directly opposite. Large and commodious bathing-houses were at once constructed and supplied from this spring, and the house now offers every facility for the comfort and convenience of invalids and pleasure-seekers, being amply furnished with all the appointments usually found in first-class hotels.

In 1871, Mr. Johnson died, and the house is now under the supervision of Messrs. Cary, Tunnicliff & Blake, heirs of the General.

THE NATIONAL HOTEL.

THIS hotel was erected by Mr. Davis Brown in 1852, who sold it to Benjamin E. Caney and Moses Jaques, in 1855. Mr. Caney soon bought out the interest of Mr. Jaques, and conducted it as a public house until his death in 1866. Mr. Caney had ten sons and four daughters, who are all now living except Charles, the fourth son, who enlisted in the 78th Regiment New York Volunteers, in the autumn of 1861, and was killed at the battle of Antietam, September 17th, 1862, and was buried on the field. He had a short time previous to his death received the appointment of captain. He was shot dead while gallantly leading his men into action.*

In January, 1863, his remains were disinterred and removed to the cemetery in this village, together with the remains of his daughter of four years, who had recently died in New York. In 1865, Mr. Alvin Barrus purchased the National Hotel, and it has been successfully conducted by him until the present time. This hotel is pleasantly situated on the north side of Main Street, and has accommodations for about sixty guests.

THE CANADARAGO HOUSE.

THIS new and commodious hotel is pleasantly situated opposite the Spring House, on Main Street, and has ample accommodations for one hundred and fifty guests.

F. STANTON, Proprietor.

* Captain Caney is the only soldier buried in this place. Mrs. Benjamin E. Caney died March 8th, 1862, in the sixty-second year of her age, being the first death in this large family.

THE INTERNATIONAL HOTEL,

ON the corner of Main and Lake Streets, has accommodations for one hundred guests.

W. E. DARROW, Proprietor.

THE CENTRAL HOTEL.

THIS house is new and pleasantly situated on the east side of Lake Street. Can accommodate sixty-five guests.

P. R. MINER, Proprietor.

THE DERTHICK HOUSE.

THIS new and elegant house is pleasantly situated on the south side of Main Street, directly opposite the Methodist Church. Can accommodate one hundred guests.

JOHN DERTHICK, Proprietor.

DAVENPORT HOUSE.

THIS popular house stands to the east of the American, on Main Street, and has accommodations for one hundred and fifty guests.

J. S. DAVENPORT, Proprietor.

PRIVATE BOARDING HOUSES.

THE TUNNICLIFF COTTAGE, Main Street. Capacity sixty guests. *C. & M. Tunnicliff*, Proprietors.

The HOSFORD HOUSE, Main Street. Capacity sixty guests. *M. K. Hosford*, Proprietor.

The TULLER HOUSE, Main Street. Capacity one hundred guests. *N. D. Jewell*, Proprietor.

The RATHBUN HOUSE, Main Street. Capacity thirty guests. *Miss H. Rathbun*, Proprietor.

The CONKLIN HOUSE, Main Street. Capacity thirty guests. *Ezra Conklin*, Proprietor.

The CARY HOUSE, Main Street. Capacity sixty guests. *George B. Cary*, Proprietor.

J. M. DERTHICK's HOUSE, Main Street. Capacity twenty guests.

The TUNNICLIFF HOUSE, Lake Street. Capacity thirty guests. *Richard Tunnicliff*, Proprietor.

The CHAMBERLIN HOUSE, Church Street. Capacity thirty guests. *C. C. Chamberlin*, Proprietor.

The GETMAN HOUSE, Church Street. Capacity twenty guests. *Hiram Getman*, Proprietor.

The ECKLER HOUSE. This house is situated on Church Street, opposite the Spring House. Has accommodations for twenty boarders. *Levi Eckler*, Proprietor.

There are many other private houses that are open to guests through the summer season.

POST-OFFICE.

THIS important institution of the village was first established here under the administration of General Jackson, in 1829, as East Richfield. James Hyde was the first Postmaster, and held the office twelve years, or until the accession of the Whig party to power under General Harrison in 1841, when he resigned in favor of E. A. Saunders, his deputy, who held the office but a few months, when Horace Manley received the regular appointment, and was succeeded by A. R. Elwood in 1842, under the administration of John Tyler. During the time that James Hyde was Postmaster, the office was kept in the old American Hotel.

In 1848, Moses Jaques was appointed under James K. Polk; held the office but a few months, when Cyrus Osborn received the appointment, and held the office until 1853, and was succeeded by James S. Davenport. In 1862, Samuel S. Edick * received the appointment under Mr. Lincoln, but resigned in 1865 in favor of E. A. Hinds, who was duly appointed and still holds the office.

"During the year 1872, this office received and sent as follows:

"*Newspapers and Letters.*

"Dailies received, 110; weeklies, 169; semi-weeklies, 21; monthlies, 67.

"Letters sent, 75,000; letters received, 80,000; letters registered, 361.

"E. A. HINDS, P. M."

* Present Judge of Otsego County.

CORPORATION.

THE village of Richfield Springs was incorporated by Act of the Legislature, passed March 30th, 1861. It embraces within its corporate limits, about one square mile, or six hundred and forty acres.

During the last twenty months, the village has been extensively drained by sewers leading from every part of the place, to the stream leading to the lake; and no town in the State enjoys a better system of sanatory regulations.

Our streets also have been put in excellent condition, and are being constantly improved under the auspices of the corporate authorities.

There are at the present time, within this corporation, 210 dwellings, 7 hotels, 15 stores, 5 churches.

PROFESSIONS.

Lawyers.

Davenport & Tennant, Parker D. Fay, J. W. Young, William Oliver.

Physicians.

Norman Getman, W. B. Crain, O. C. Orendorf.

Magistrates.

A. R. Elwood, J. L. Comstock.

Dentists.

W. T. Bailey, T. H. Bradish.

Surveyors.

J. L. Comstock, E. W. Badger.

Teachers.

E. D. Harrington, Miss Emma Getman; Select School, Mrs. M. E. King.

Insurance Agents.

W. D. Griffin, J. D. Ibbotson, M. Tuller, L. M. Doubleday.

Notaries Public.

J. S. Davenport, M. Bryan, E. A. Hinds.

Veterinary Surgeon.

Allen S. Buchanan.

Artists.

N. S. Bowdish, F. M. Zoller, G. H. Bronner.

Banking House.

Elwood & Tuller.

BUSINESS PLACES, *March*, 1874.

Printing Office.—Richfield Springs Mercury; C. Ackerman, Editor.

Dry-Good Stores.—Elwood & Tuller, E. A. Hinds, F. Stanton.

Hardware and Stoves.—Robert Buchanan.

Hardware and Groceries.—McCredy Brothers.

Drug Stores.—A. J. Smith & Son, J. F. Getman.

Clothing Stores.—J. McCredy & Son, O. Knapp, F. C. Hunt.

Groceries.—J. Frink & Co., R. Russell.

Jewelers.—J. & H. C. Walter, J. Straus, and H. Greenman.

Grist and Flouring Mills.—John Dana.

Steam Saw-Mill.—J. Backus & Co.

Photograph Gallery.—George H. Bronner.

Book Store, Telegraph and Express Office.—James A. Storer.

Expressman.—Thomas Shoemaker.

Butter Dealer.—Peter Allen.

Cabinet Shops.—S. Palmer, Martin & Harrington.

Shoe Stores.—Guy Kinne, Jay Winne.

Farm Produce and Groceries.—P. Langdon.

Lumber Yard and Feed Store.—W. B. Ward.

Butchers and Cattle Dealers.—Vroman & Brown.

Harness Shops.—C. B. Fuller.

Tin Shops.—R. Buchanan, H. Royston.

Barber.—G. H. Thomson.

Carriage Makers.—A. Barker, H. J. Freudenberg.

Blacksmiths.—A. Allen & Son, R. J. Dutcher, Mr. Shimmel.

Painters.—A. C. Cole, J. Horn, and G. H. Johnson.

Carpenters.—Twenty.

"THE RICHFIELD SPRINGS MERCURY."

THE first number of the Mercury was published, July 19th, 1867, by Henry L. Brown. Mr. Brown continued its publication until October 22d, 1868, when he sold the office to its present proprietor, Mr. C. Ackerman, Mr. Ackerman inspired new life in the office, and January 21st, 1871, enlarged the Mercury from a 24-by-36, to 26-by-40 sheet, and made large additions to the office.

In the spring of 1873, he purchased one of C. Potter & Co.'s power-presses, and to-day has one of the best country offices in the State. The Mercury has nearly one thousand subscribers.

The jobbing department of this establishment is first-class, and its work is seldom excelled by the best city offices. The present firm, C. Ackerman & Son, are en-joying the confidence of the people, and doing all in their power to promote the prosperity of our village, and to advance the moral tone of the people.

MASONIC LODGE.

RICHFIELD SPRINGS LODGE No. 482, Free and Accepted Masons, was duly organized on the 12th day of August, 1859, by W. M. Mordecai Myers, Past Grand Master of the Grand Lodge of the State of New York.

First Officers.—Hon. James Hyde, W. M.; Hon. Charles Delong, S. W.; Daniel H. Woodbury, J. W.; Lot H. Hasford, Secretary; Gen. Wm. P. Johnson, Treas-urer; David Firman, J. D.; Silas Gray, Tiler.

This Lodge holds its regular communications on the 2d and 4th Saturday in each month. Present mem-bership about one hundred.

Present Officers, 1873.—Martin Goes, W. M.; John F. Getman, S. W.; J. A. Storer, J. W.; N. S. Bowdish, S. D.; Menzo Barrus, J. D.; A. H. Elwood, Sec.; N. Getman, Treas.; T. I. Jaques, Tiler. Lodge rooms in Walter's Block, Main Street.

Ladies' Degrees.—The Initial Degree for ladies was conferred August 13th, 1859, on the following names, by Mr. M. Benedict, viz.: Mary Cheeseman, Mary Johnson, Matilda Reed, Olive Elwood, Fanny Hyde. The following ladies received the degree of "*True Kinsman*": Matilda Reed, Fanny Hyde.

RICHFIELD SPRINGS, CHAPTER No. 222.

First Officers.—This sublime adjunct of Masonry was organized April 29th, 1868. S. R. Stewart, H. P.; L. M. Doubleday, S.; W. B. Lidell, K.

Present Officers.—N. S. Bowdish, H. P.; C. Crim, S.; W. A. Smith, R. A. C.; A. H. Elwood, Third V.; M. Barrus, First V.; J. A. Storer, Treasurer; J. F. Getman, K.; E. A. Hinds, C. of H.; S. R. Ward, P. S.; James A. Storer, Second V.; John Derthick, Secretary; T. I. Jaques, Tiler. Present number of members, seventy-one. Regular convocations, first and third Friday of each month.

THE CIRCULATING LIBRARY.

THIS association was first organized by the ladies of this village in the spring of 1860, with eleven members, at two dollars each. The books purchased were rented at the rate of ten cents per volume for one week, and the money so obtained applied to the purchase of new books.

The price of membership has been raised from time to time, and is fixed at the present date at *ten dollars*.

The number of volumes now in the library is nine hundred and thirty, consisting chiefly of works of fiction, but comprising also essays, travels, poems, and biographies.

The new and popular works of each season are obtained as soon as issued, making a delightful resource to visitors who do not desire to burden themselves with the care and weight of books.

THE TELEGRAPH.

Previous to the year 1862, the communication of Richfield Springs with the outside world, was limited to a daily mail to Herkimer by stage-coach. The growing importance of the village rendered this inadequate to the needs of the place, and a few public-spirited citizens, with a view rather to the benefit of the village than for profit to themselves, conceived the idea of building a telegraph line to Herkimer, thus placing us on an equal footing with more favored " watering-places." The citizens of the village promptly subscribed the necessary amount, about one thousand dollars, and operations were immediately begun. The Richfield Springs and Herkimer Telegraph Company was organized under the laws of the State of New York, October 4th, 1861. The capital stock consisted of thirty-six shares of $25 each. The following were the first directors: Jacob Allen, William P. Johnson, J. S. Davenport, Morgan Bryan, and James C. Armstrong.

William P. Johnson was chosen President, and James Hyde, Secretary. The material for the line was purchased at once, and constructed during the autumn, and opened for business January 6th, 1862.

William R. Tunnicliff was the first operator, his office

being in the building known as Washington Hall, which has since been metamorphosed into the elegant summer hotel called the "Canadarago House." The line was of great benefit to the village, and the stimulus given to all business by the war, was shared also by the telegraph line, which continued to do a good *business*.

The success and utility of the Richfield Springs and Herkimer Telegraph Line created a desire for its extension to Cooperstown; and a separate company was formed in 1864, for this purpose.

The principal movers in this enterprise were the members of the Richfield Springs and Herkimer Telegraph Company. The Richfield Springs and Cooperstown Telegraph Company was organized February 2d, 1864, and the following officers chosen:—*Directors:* A. R. Elwood, Morgan Bryan, Alfred Chamberlin, and James S. Davenport, of Richfield Springs; and William E. Corey, of Cooperstown. Alfred Chamberlin was subsequently chosen President, and A. R. Elwood, Secretary and Treasurer. The line was built *via* Springfield Centre and Otsego Lake, and was constructed in a substantial manner. The two lines were united in the Richfield Springs office, and were worked in one circuit, although the business was separated. The stocks of both companies were gradually absorbed by Alfred Chamberlin and A. R. Elwood, and consolidated February 15th, 1867, under the style of the Richfield Springs Telegraph Company; with lines extending from Cooperstown through Springfield Centre, Richfield Springs, and Mohawk, to Herkimer, a distance of thirty-one miles.

The Western Union Telegraph Company had in the meantime added a wire from Herkimer to Utica, making the latter point the repeating station for the Richfield Springs line, thus greatly facilitating the dispatch of business. November 15th, 1865, the Richfield Springs line was leased to the Western Union Telegraph Company, for the term of *ten* years, which company had a wire then extending from Palatine Bridge to Sharon Springs, which was by agreement further extended *via* Cherry Valley to Cooperstown, where they were united, forming a continuous circuit from Albany to Syracuse, *via* Sharon, Cooperstown, Richfield Springs, and Herkimer.

In 1871, the Western Union Company constructed a line from Utica to Richfield Springs along the railroad, *via* "Richfield Junction" and West Winfield, thus doubling the facilities of this office, which are unexcelled by any village of its size in the country.

William R. Tunnicliff, the first operator and manager, died in 1865, and was succeeded by James A. Storer, who has held the position to the present time.

RAILROAD.

The Utica, Chenango and Susquehanna Valley Railroad Company, was organized under the General Railroad Act, early in the year 1866, running from Utica to Sherburne in Chenango County; also a branch deflecting from the main line at a point $13\frac{1}{2}$ miles south of Utica, and running thence *via* Richfield Springs to a connection with the Albany and Susquehanna Railroad, at Colliersville on the Susquehanna River. A law authorizing the city of Utica to issue bonds and take stock in the road to the amount of $500,000, passed February 19th, 1866.

A law authorizing the several towns along the line of the road to issue bonds and take stock, was passed

April 4th, 1866. Work was immediately commenced, and the road was completed to Waterville, twenty-one miles, in the autumn of 1867; and to Sherburne forty-three miles, about the 15th of August, 1868.

In the mean time, efforts were made to bond the town of Bridgewater on the Richfield branch, without success, and fears were entertained that this part of the enterprise would be a failure, until about the first of January, 1868, when the obstacles were removed, and the bonding of the towns along the line of the branch was pushed forward by the Financial Agent of the company, Ezra W. Badger, Esq.* On the first of June following, this work was completed as far as Richfield Springs.

The amount of funds provided by the several towns being insufficient to complete the road to the Springs, the company called for fifty thousand dollars more, and over thirty-five thousand was promptly subscribed by citizens of Richfield Springs and vicinity; and the work of grading was begun; and on the first day of June, 1870, the road was opened from Utica to Richfield Springs, by the Delaware, Lackawanna, and Western Railroad Company; that company having leased the whole road, a few months previous. The terminus of the road at this time was three-fourths of a mile west of the village, on the direct line as surveyed down the valley. And as the D. L. & W. R. R. Co. abandoned the extension in that direction, it was decided that the terminus be removed to a more convenient point. The village corporation was bonded for thirty thousand dollars for that purpose; and about the middle of May, 1871, the D. L. & W. Company broke ground for the

---

* The success of this important enterprise is due, to a very great extent, to the personal efforts and direct agency of Mr. Badger, who is now a resident of Richfield Springs.

extension, and on the fourth day of July following, trains were run into the village. This enterprise has proved a successful investment. Two trains now leave this place daily and return.

Through the summer months, express trains come through from New York, without change of cars, arriving at Richfield about 7 P. M.

Conductors.—Major D. F. Everett, Charles Farrell.

Engineers.—L. T. Hewett, Fred. Eastman.

Tickets Agent.—J. D. Ibbotson.

Baggagemen.—W. A. Swift, W. H. Chapman.

THE RAILWAY STATION

Is always a point of deep interest, especially at a watering-place, for here all classes congregate—some to greet expected guests or relatives, some to see their friends off on the train, while others seem to be led by idle curiosity to witness the arrival and departure of trains, or gaze upon those who are actively engaged in business incident to travel. Here we witness the warm and earnest greetings and civilities interchanged by friends long separated, and, not unfrequently, the tearful separation perhaps of others, that a few hours will carry many hundred miles apart.

The railway station of Richfield Springs is situated on the west side of Lake Street, in the southern part of the village, and but a few moments' walk or ride to all the *hotels*, from which a line of omnibuses run to and from every train.

4

THE CEMETERY.

THE old burying-ground adjacent to the Presbyterian Church in this village, was presented to the public as a burial-place, by Nathan Dow, Esq., about the year 1825. It comprises about one acre of land, and contains at the present time 265 visible graves.

The first interment in this grave-yard was a grandchild of Mr. Dow. The ground is pleasantly shaded by a vigorous growth of young maples, and other varieties of ornamental forest-trees. A new cemetery, outside the bounds·of the corporation, was long contemplated ; and in 1871, the village trustees purchased of William P. Johnson eight acres of land on a beautifully elevated ridge, a short distance to the southeast of the village.

These grounds have a southern slope, overlooking the lake and Canadarago Valley to the south. It is now known as " Lakeview Cemetery."

About one-half the ground has been surveyed into lots twenty feet square, with intervening avenues.

Several interments have already been made here ; and the present neglected condition of the old burying-ground will no doubt induce those having friends buried there, to remove their remains to the new cemetery. A receiving vault is now the great need of these new grounds.

We trust the grounds of the old cemetery will ultimately be converted into a public park.

CANADARAGO LAKE, *from Perkins' Hill.*

CANADARAGO LAKE.

THIS lake lies about three-fourths of a mile directly south from Richfield Springs, is five miles in extreme length, and from one to one and a half miles in width. It is nearly surrounded by wood-covered hills or mountain-ranges, with intervening fields and highly cultivated farms. This is one of the most beautiful of the small lakes of the State, and abounds in a great variety of most excellent fish, that furnish abundant piscatorial sport for those who visit this place through the warm summer season. At the time of the early settlement of this region, salt-water fish were occasionally found in its waters, but this is now prevented by the numerous dams built across the stream leading to it. A small steamboat was placed upon this lake in the summer of 1872, as a pleasure-boat. The annual appropriation which our State Legislature has made for several years for the propagation of fish in the lakes of the State, is certainly a matter of important consideration.

Over 100,000 young fish have been put in this lake during the past winter, by Professor Green, of Rochester. About one-tenth of the number were trout, the balance white-fish.

A beautifully wooded Island, comprising about seven acres, and lying high above the water, rests within the bosom of this lake, its dark and cooling shades having long been a place of popular resort for pleasure parties as indicated by dates carved in the bark of trees. (This Island is now the private property of Mr. E. A. Ward, of New York.) A corresponding Island once stood directly to the west of this, but about the commencement of this century, it suddenly disappeared by

sinking far down beneath the waters of the lake.* It is
said that the tops of large trees can now be seen, still
standing erect, far down in the transparent waters. The
following Indian tradition in relation to this island, has
been handed down to us: "A famous healing Indian
prophet once dwelt upon a beautiful island in the midst
of Canadarago Lake, to whom invalids from all the Iroquois used to come, and leave their maladies. At midnight he would glide softly away in his canoe, penetrate
the dark forest to the fountains, and then return to his
patients with vessels full of the magic waters.

"By his great success he became proud and powerful ; and at last he called himself the twin brother of the
Great Spirit. This blasphemy kindled the anger of the
Almighty, and it consumed the boaster. One morning
when a bridal party went thither to receive the prophet's
blessing, the island had disappeared. The Great Spirit
in his wrath had thrust it with the proud prophet so deep
into the earth, that the waters of the lake where it stood
are unfathomable by human measurement."

THE SUNKEN ISLAND.

BY ETHEL LYNN.

O'er Canadarago the shadows creep,
Dreams of her silent summer sleep ;
Yon pictured hill, a blue-veined lid,
Curtains the brightness beneath it hid ;
The toying tress of the willow swings,
And the tasselled birch her guerdon flings,
Till the wave wakes up from its revery,
And, Indian-like, laughs silently.

---

* This is a veritable fact, within the recollection of our oldest
citizens. It will be observed that Canadarago Lake on the west,
and the Otsego Lake on the east, form the extreme sources of the
Susquehanna River.

In-shore the tall flags moveless stand,
With lances straight like warder band,
To guard the lily's jewelled cup,
Whose golden wine the wave bears up;
But guards in vain: the robber bee
Drinks and away, humming merrily;
And the dragon-fly waves its wing of light
Into the sunshine and out of sight.

But just where the mountain shadows break
Lies the sunken isle of the laughing lake,
Where the soft, green rushes idly sway,
And the fisher's boat is seen alway,
As the angler peers through the limpid wave
For a glimpse of the island's lonely grave,
And dreams of the time when in air it stood,
With its crown of flowers and belt of wood.

For Canadarago a legend keeps,
To be whispered low when the midnight creeps
Moonless and still on the lonely shore,
A tale of the Lost for evermore.
Far back in the land of the Long Ago,
Stood an island fair in the summer glow,
Where ever alone a prophet dwelt,
For whose healing touch the suffering knelt.

Thither the Mohawk warrior came,
With the wound from poison-dart aflame;
And the Iroquois, with his war-won pain,
Sought at his hand for health again.
Savage of mien and dark of mood,
As well became his Indian blood;
Sullen and stern, none ever guessed
The secrets locked in his dusky breast:

Knew not how oft in the swift canoe
The shivered waves from the paddles flew,
As close by the dim, deep forest stayed,
The prophet's foot in the darkness strayed,
Till close by the bitter fountain's brink
He stopped at last, yet not to drink;
But bore from thence the wondrous draught,
The source and secret of his craft.

At last, the olden legend saith,
He claimed the power to conquer Death;
And spoke in horrid blasphemy
Of twinship with Divinity;
Then the Great Spirit's awful frown
Sent isle and prophet hurtling down;
And wondering pilgrims to that shore
Saw isle or prophet never more.

The Sunken Island!—Ah, 'twere well
If only legends wild could tell
The tale. On Life's broad sea
Such things as these there often be;
Bright spots that softly shine and gleam,
Fair as a sinless angel's dream;
And yet they sink—and all but we
Go floating on right merrily.

So each alone his secrets keeps,
Where his lost vision bides and sleeps;
Sails bravely on and makes no moan,
Over the fairy landscape gone;
Yet glancing where the rushes grow,
Bent by the breath of the Long Ago,
He says no word, but dreams the while
Of the unforgotten Sunken Isle.

CANADARAGO VALLEY.

LEADING southward from the lake is the picturesque
valley of the Canadarago, through which flows the little
stream known as " Oaks Creek," that winds its peaceful
way through the dark shades of the primitive forest, that
reaches far down into the valley from the mountain-
range on the east. The ride along the base of this
mountain in the summer months is extremely delightful, being beautifully embowered beneath the out-stretch-
ed arms of gigantic forest-trees, that shade the way for
many miles, for here the wild birds are filling the forest

with the sweetest of music—the thrushes and robins, and the multitude of feathered songsters, each of whom has his little note to add to the chorus, till to greet the rising sun and the waking world, rises such a gush of melody, that the listener stands enraptured in the midst of these evidences of Divine goodness,

" With the brooklet's merry murmur
In the gloomy wood,
Birdlike music lightly breaking
Through the solitude."

Along this romantic way, we occasionally pass a " log-cabin." These ancient landmarks of pioneer life are usually found unoccupied and falling to decay. There is something peculiarly interesting in these relics of the early settlement of our country. There is no doubt an interesting history associated with them, although it may be forever lost in oblivion ; nevertheless, we can look upon them with sentiments of the deepest interest, and revert to the days of their prime, when occupied by the hardy pioneer, with his deep forest surroundings, far removed from the previous social pleasures and priv-ileges of the more thickly settled valleys of New Eng-land, from which many of the early settlers of this region removed.

In these rude and humble abodes, many of our most eminent and distinguished men first saw the light of life ; here taught in early childhood to contend with the stern realities of primitive days, they learned the lessons of patient endurance, persevering toil, and self-reliance that so eminently fitted them for their future triumphs in private and public life. And the relative mental and physical vigor of the age, typified by these ancient relics, and the present, is a theme worthy the grave attention of the moralist.

LEROY, OR SCHUYLER'S LAKE VILLAGE,

Is pleasantly located at the southern end or foot of Canadarago Lake, and has a fixed population of about three hundred. It has two churches, two public houses, stores, shops, and other places of business usually found in villages of its size. John Tunnicliff kept the first store and public house soon after the close of the Revolution. About the commencement of the present century, Eliphalet Brockway kept a public house, and M. Cushman opened a store about the same time. John Hartshorn built the first grist-mill on Herkimer Creek. The first church (Episcopal) was built at this place near the close of the last century. As the New York Gazetteer says, "Rev. Daniel Nash was the first pastor, in 1797." According to the same authority, Hendrick Herkimer settled near the lake on Herkimer Creek, prior to the Revolution, or about the time that John Tunnicliff occupied his purchase two miles to the southward. According to history, the Herkimer family maintain a prominent position in the annals of Herkimer County, during the struggle for American Independence. Mr. N. S. Benton, in his history, says, "Although a little out of the order of events, I will here give all the information I have been able to collect in regard to the surviving branches of the family of General Herkimer.

"Of the four brothers who remained in the country and attached to the Revolutionary cause, Nicholas and John died without issue. George left two sons, John and Joseph, who have been dead a number of years. Joseph left one son only, who until very recently resided at Little Falls. Henry left five sons, Joseph, Nicholas, Abraham, George, and Henry. I have not been able to trace out the descendants of Joseph and Nicholas. Abraham removed to Pennsylvania, where his descendants are now to be found. George, the general's nephew, left four sons, Henry G., Timothy, and George, who in 1854 lived in Otsego County, near Schuyler's Lake, and William, who had removed to Chautauqua County. The general's nephew Henry left Joseph, Henry, and Robert II. The first named of these three brothers lived in Springfield, Otsego County, in 1854, and the two latter emigrated to Michigan some years ago," etc.

A family by the name of Schuyler built a cabin on the bank of Herkimer Creek in 1774, where they resided during the Revolutionary War, who, by maintaining a strict neutrality, were permitted to live undisturbed by the marauding bands of hostile savages that infested the forests between this point and the Mohawk valley. A system of espionage was early established, as the safety of the frontier settlers required a knowledge of the Indian movements on the part of the military forces in this vicinity. Abraham Herkimer, a soldier, stationed at Fort Herkimer, was chosen by the commanding officer to scout the forests in the vicinity of Canadarago Lake, and watch the movements of a large party of Indians under the lead of the notorious Brant, who were known to be prowling in that region for the purpose of rapine and the most heartless cruelties. Alone he penetrated the deep forest, through which he wandered during the day in its wild solitudes, and at nightfall found himself at or near a point in what is now the town of Exeter, where the Deerlick Creek flows into the Herkimer, when he suddenly came upon a formidable party of war-painted savages, surrounding a blazing fire, dancing wildly, and brandishing the gleaming blades of their blood-stained knives over their heads, with an occasional yell of fiendish exultation, in view of their murderous mission. With emotions of trepidation, he silently withdrew to a place of safety, and passed the night in sleepless fear, but determined if possible to ascertain their movements on the following morning.

At the early dawn of day, they were observed to retire in the direction of the Canadarago, thence to the eastward toward Otsego Lake and Cherry Valley.* This movement was immediately made known to the commanding officer of the fort, who at once dispatched a messenger to the last-named place, but too late to avert the fate that had already befallen it, as will be seen under the head of Cherry Valley. Soon after the adventure of Herkimer, another scout, by the name of Smith, volunteered to visit the same region, and, if possible, penetrate the valley south of Canadarago Lake. The first day he reached the cabin of Mr. Schuyler at Herkimer Creek, where he remained over night. Early the next morning, he proceeded over the trail to the stream leading from the lake (Oaks Creek), and upon approaching its western bank, found the trail obstructed by a fallen tree. While looking for a passage around this obstruction, his eye suddenly detected the dusky forms of two Indians approaching from the opposite direction. He at once discovered that he had been seen by the savages, who were well armed, and escape was impossible. The guns of Smith and the Indians were simultaneously levelled, but a well-directed bullet from the rifle of the former sent one of the Indians reeling to the ground, with a death-whoop that struck terror to the heart of Smith, who quickly fled, retracing his steps to the cabin

---

* A Mrs. House, living near Little Lakes, whose husband was a Tory, learning of their approach, fled alone through the forest to Cherry Valley to apprise them of approaching danger.

of Schuyler, where he related the adventure. He remained here but a few moments, however, being advised to fly for his life, as a large party were supposed to be in that vicinity, and his capture would be immediately attempted by the enraged savages. Taking the trail leading northward, he ran nearly the entire distance to Fort Herkimer; and was so greatly exhausted by this extreme exercise, that he died in less than two weeks thereafter. In the afternoon of the day of the occurrence just related, several Indians visited the cabin of Mr. Schuyler, and reported to him the sad fate of their comrade, and at their urgent solicitation he accompanied them to the spot, and there saw the lifeless body. The ball had entered the right eye, and passed entirely through the head, causing almost instant death. He assisted in burying the Indian's body near the place where it fell.

The most direct Indian trail from the valley of the Mohawk to this lake, led from the vicinity of Little Falls to South Columbia direct, thence deflecting from the valley to the summit of "Gunset Hill." This eminence was a great place of resort of the hostile bands of Indians during the Revolution, as it commands an extensive view of the entire valley of the Canadarago south to the Susquehanna River. It was known as the "Indian Lookout." Traces of the trail leading to it can now be seen. It derives its name from the circumstance that guns were set by the early hunters at this point in such a manner as to be easily discharged by the approach of wild animals. Gunset Hill is situated directly to the west of Richfield Springs, and is the extreme northern spur of the range of mountains bordering the valley of the Canadarago and Susquehanna on the west, and from it we obtain a fine view of the entire village and surroundings.

THE HON. WILLIAM CULLEN CRAIN.

The road leading northerly through the neighboring villages of Cullen and Jordanville, towards the old German settlement of Andrustown, has long been for the visitors of Richfield a favorite drive. It lies in a sequestered but pretty district of rich farming lands, the graceful undulations of which, together with scattered vineyards of hops and fine forest-trees, resemble and even rival the handsomest portions of Kent and Surrey in England. On this road, and near the spot where the waters of the " Ocquionis " Creek issue from the ground, is " Cullenwood," an unpretending but tasteful country-seat of the olden style. This for a period of nearly sixty years was the home of William Cullen Crain; a name prominently associated with the history of this beautiful region. Of the numerous visitors to Richfield in past years, there were comparatively few who did not carry to their homes recollections of pleasant hours passed at " Cullenwood ;" for here, in the language of a prominent journal, " Colonel Crain administered a courtly and elegant hospitality, which will never be forgotten by those who shared it."

The social and personal characteristics of Colonel Crain were indeed such as would have made him a marked man in any community.

He was born in the town of Warren, Herkimer County, August 31st, 1795. His father, Rufus Crain, is mentioned in " Benton's Herkimer County and Upper Mohawk Valley," as a skilful physician, a near relative of General Israel Putnam, and as having held the office of Judge of the Court of Common Pleas for sixteen years.

The early education of William Cullen Crain was

intrusted to the Rev. John P. Spinner,* whose agency
in forming the character and developing that elegant
manner which so distinguished his pupil in after life was
most marked. We read of Mr. Spinner, that " he was a
graduate of the University of Mentz, and that during
his six years' collegiate probation, he passed through a
thorough course of studies in philosophy, mathematics,
history, languages ancient and modern, divinity, jurisprudence, and medicine. He was tall in stature, digni-
fied in deportment, and polished in his manners. He
possessed a capacious and vigorous mind. With the
ancient and most of the modern continental languages,
and especially the French, Spanish, and Italian, he was
quite as familiar as with his own native German." We
may add that Dominie Spinner was as well and favorably
known to the population of Herkimer as a minister of
the Gospel, as was his contemporary, Priest Nash, to the
people of Otsego. After leaving the family of Mr. Spinner, young Crain pursued the study of the classics until
prepared to enter the senior class at *Yale*, which it was
then his intention to do ; circumstances, however, induced
him to change his mind, and he entered his father's
office as a student of medicine, and practised for about
two years.† His boyhood during the time not occupied
by studies, was chiefly spent among the German settlers
of Andrustown. From early associations, there grew up
between him and those settlers relations of friendship

---

* Father of Hon. F. E. Spinner, of Washington.

† On one occasion, towards the spring of the year, accompanying
his father on horseback for the purpose of visiting a patient on the
westerly side of Canadarago Lake, being assured by the messenger
who had come for them, that it was entirely safe, they crossed the
lake on the ice at a point near the island Returning in about three
hours after, they found that the ice had been completely broken up
by the action of the east wind

and mutual respect, never afterwards in any degree affected or diminished. In after years, many of those inimitable stories of the Colonel, which so delighted and convulsed with laughter his listeners, were reminiscences of his youth spent among these Germans. For these people he had a real admiration, and often contrasted the simplicity of their manners and the mutual confidence subsisting between them in their business transactions, with the distrust and the more artful character of their Yankee neighbors. As an illustration of this, we have heard the Colonel say, that among these Germans, promissory notes were then almost unknown, the simple word of the borrower being considered ample security.

These Teutons, between whom and the subject of our sketch there existed such a strong bond of sympathy, are in fact a sterling race; and to this day the customs of their ancestors and their national language is sacredly *preserved.*

The "Settlement," for by that appellation Andrustown is still known, is only distant an hour's drive from the Springs, and the visitor here will be well repaid by making it the special object of a day's excursion.

The ancestors of the Andrustown settlers, the Hoyers, Crims, Bells, and others, were a portion of that Protestant band, which, at the close of the seventeenth, and beginning of the eighteenth centuries, were driven from their homes in the Palatinate by the persecutions of the Romish hierarchy. Queen Anne, of England, deeply sympathizing with these exiles, with whose prince she was nearly related, furnished to them, in the year 1708, at the expense of her government, ships for their conveyance to the colony of New York. They penetrated into the County of Herkimer, as early as the year 1723, and there is reason to believe that the Andrustown colony dates its existence from that period. It is interesting to note that shoe-buckles, pipes, combs, and various ornaments worn and used by these refugees from the Palatinate, are still preserved in the families of their descendants. In 1826, Colonel Crain married Miss Perses Narina Tunnicliff, daughter of William Tunnicliff, Esq., and granddaughter of the Count George Ernst August Von Ranzau, an officer on the staff of the Baron Von Riedesel, and author of the interesting Journal of Burgoyne's Expedition contained in the archives of the great general staff at Berlin. His landed interests in Warren being considerable, Colonel Crain now gave up the practice of medicine, and devoted himself to agriculture, of which he was a real lover. Through successive years he did much to improve the breeds of cattle in this part of the State, and early brought hither imported stock. But these occupations were not permitted to interfere with his literary pursuits.

He was an extensive reader, literally a devourer of books. His memory was remarkable, and it is much to be regretted that the information he possessed in regard to the local traditions of Warren, were not by him committed to writing for the edification of those who survive him. We have heard the Colonel say, that the creek which issues from the ground at Cullen, and discharges itself into Ward's Lake in this village, was by the Indians called the "Ocquionis," and we trust that this name may be revived; and it would not be inappropriate to apply it to the street now known as *Church Street*. We shall here also rescue from oblivion a singular fact in connection with this stream, related by the Colonel, who received it from the venerable Paul Crim, of Andrustown, than whom there could be no more truthful witness. Crim told the Colonel that he had frequently, when a boy, fished with the Indians at the source of the Ocquionis at Cullen, and that he had caught beautiful salmon, and in large quantities, there. It was a great fishing-place for the Indians, and the absence of all dams between that point and the Chesapeake Bay, permitted these fish to penetrate thus far at times of high water. Richard Schooley, who nearly reached his one-hundredth year, and who was noted as a hunter and trapper, also told the Colonel that he had seen, on the subsidence of the waters of this creek, thousands of these fish dead in its bed ; and on one occasion he saw a number of bears feeding upon them. With all the incidents of the bloody massacre of the Andrustown colonists by the Indians under Brant, in the month of July, 1775, the Colonel was also familiar. We have heard him relate that on this occasion, the Indians having killed one Bell, carried away captive to Canada his son, then about two years old, and that this child was retained by the savages in their wilderness home about ten years. When eventually restored to his family, the traits and character of the Indian were so thoroughly stamped upon the boy as to be irremovable, notwithstanding all efforts of the family. Though induced for a time to wear the garb of the white man, he would stealthily don the Indian costume, and betake himself to the woods to fish and hunt.

His uncle accompanying him in a boat on one of these fishing excursions, and not guiding the boat exactly in a manner to please this disciple of the aborigines, the boy immediately took from the bottom of the boat a loaded gun, and pointing it at the uncle, threatened him with instant death if he did not guide the boat differently. This boy, not being able to adapt himself to civilized life, or wean his affections from his friends of the forest, became moody and melancholy, and soon died.

Nothing could be more entertaining than to listen to Colonel Crain's recital of the early history of this neighborhood. He had received the facts from the generation who were themselves participators therein ; and nothing that had been told to him, ever escaped his remarkable memory. His colloquial powers were of the first order, and his social disposition led him to take great pleasure in imparting incidents of the past to others. The Colonel was through life an ardent Democrat of the Jeffersonian school. Few men have been more thoroughly imbued with the principles and doctrines of the Democratic party. They seemed to impart a directing influence to the actions of his life ; and he had a thorough conviction that they were necessary to the growth, prosperity, and welfare of our country. For many years he occupied a prominent position in the field of politics. He filled with honor many places of distinction and trust, and exerted throughout a marked influence within his party. He was three times a member of the State Legislature ; in 1832, 1845, and 1846.

During the last term, he was Speaker of the Assembly, a position which he filled with eminent dignity and ability.

He was a candidate for the State Senate in 1857, and in 1860 was the candidate of the united Democracy for Lieutenant-Governor. He represented the Democracy many times in Democratic national conventions; was several times Presidential elector upon the Democratic ticket, and often represented his party in State conventions. It was in the capacity of a presiding officer over various deliberative bodies that Colonel Crain's peculiar fitness and easy dignity rendered him most conspicuous. So true is this, that we are told by those who were present, that no one can call to mind the Legislative

session of 1846, without a vivid recollection of the urbane
and satisfactory manner in which the chair was filled
by the portly person of the Hon. William C. Crain.
The writer well remembers personally more than once
observing the Colonel as he entered some hall where were
assembled the delegates of his party in convention—
how his very aspect and carriage seemed to suggest him
as the proper man to occupy the chair; a suggestion
which was seldom lost ; for when present, he was exceedingly apt to be nominated and elected by *acclaim.* It
was on one occasion of this kind that he exhibited that
happy facility of resource which distinguished him, and
often turned seemingly embarrassing emergencies to his
own advantage. To appreciate the incident, it will be
necessary to state that his was a person of ponderous
and liberal dimensions, a face glowing with genial intelligence, an elevated dome of thought—a *tout ensemble*
bespeaking "a living minister of gratitude to the boun-
ties of the earth, and the fullness thereof." It occurred
at the conventions of the two rival factions of the Democratic party at Syracuse in 1856. After the two factions had harmonized and united, forming one body,
Colonel Crain was called to the chair. On attempting
to take his seat, however, it was discovered that the chair
was not capacious enough to contain the portly person
of the chairman. This, of course, was the cause of some
merriment; but so far from being disconcerted, the
Colonel immediately rose and said, "Gentlemen, how
can you expect that one chair will be large enough to
contain the chairman of two conventions ? "

Colonel Crain was alike a gentleman and a politician
of the old school. His chief political services were performed at a time when integrity and economy in public
affairs were at least the rule, and not the exception, and

when his own party was most successful in its efforts to supply these principles to the administration of the government. Says one of the journals, " Together with Silas Wright, Michael Hoffman, Colonel Young, and others, Colonel Crain labored to bring about the convention of 1846, which gave to the State in the main its present Constitution. He and the patriotic statesmen with whom he co-operated, had procured many substantial reforms and closed many avenues of expenditure. The unlimited power of the Legislature to create debt, presented to their minds a most formidable danger, which nothing but a constitutional limitation could avert. To ' pay as you go,' was their rule of political economy, and they endeavored to incorporate that rule into the organic law. These efforts to a large extent succeeded. But inasmuch as we have seen, in the subsequent workings of our State government, much of corruption and maladministration, it is to be remembered that the authors of these efforts at amendment are not to be held responsible. It is not to be forgotten, that those who labored for the call of the convention sought to avert by the wisest provisions the very evils from which we have since suffered. They demanded limitations and restraints upon the debt-making power of the Legislature, checks upon expenditure, the abolition of useless offices, and a rigid economy in administration. These objects in their full scope and bearing they were unable to achieve by the final action of the convention when assembled ; and hence have arisen most of the mischiefs which we have since experienced. Although space will not be allowed us to dwell upon this and other kindred subjects, enough has transpired since to fully vindicate the wisdom and foresight of these sterling patriots and leaders in the Democratic cause."

Of course, as a result of his long political career, Colonel Crain was intimately associated with many of the chief political leaders of the State and nation.

Among his warm friends were Silas Wright, Azariah C. Flagg, William L. Marcy, John Van Buren, and many others, several of whom still live to attest his worth. Their friendship was a common cohesion in a common cause. In fact, it was in the social sphere, and there alone, that Colonel Crain was really to be known in his inmost nature; and his success and popularity even with his own party were in our humble judgment greatly due to his social qualities, to the geniality of his disposition, and the cordial and gentlemanly warmth of his address. He was pre-eminently a man of popular manners, and had he been swayed by an ambition commensurate with his power to please, it were difficult to assign limits to his career of popularity. But one of his most remarkable traits was a seeming freedom from selfish ambition. He scarcely put forth an effort of his own for office; he was not a political knight of the "golden spur," and never bought one jot of his way to station or emolument. Besides, his insinuating address was not attended by its too frequent parasites, intrigue and duplicity. With him everything was open, generous, manly; that which he seemed to be, that he was, a gentleman. It has been said of him that during one session of the Legislature, while measures affecting State finances were much under consideration, a brother member said to him, in allusion to one of these: "Colonel, we shall have to study a little 'finesse,' to get that thing through." "Sir," was the reply, "I think we had better study finance, than finesse." It is said that finesse is unknown to a liberal mind; certainly he never managed for his own preferment. He simply clung to his principles and creed, and wherever

the *vox populi* decreed he should go, thither he went,
but aspired no further. While others were laboring
against head-winds on the sea of politics, seeking for car-
goes of the coveted " loaves and fishes," he remained pas-
sive; or in his choice of place, anchored upon his own
home—yes, his own quiet home, which he could make
so happy, and which those who visited it can well remember was such an abode of elegant and courtly hospitality;
not that it vied in splendor with many of the more
costly abodes of modern luxury. It was the man that
distinguished the place, not the place the man; and he
never starved comfort to feed pride. Here it was that
Colonel Crain could be known as he was, and where those
who knew him will never forget him. Here the guests
of Richfield often resorted to him; here all, of high and
low degree, received his courteous kindness, while, with
a manner truly patrician, he asserted his title of a true
Democrat. One of the critics of human nature holds
that men of business make their movements in straight or
direct lines; men of leisure, in curved or graceful lines.
Certainly the Colonel was a man of considerable leisure,
and as certainly one of uncommon politeness and grace
of demeanor, although a countryman by taste and education; at once a Cincinnatus and a Chesterfield. Yet
this was not all: he was a man of unusual powers of
conversation; though at times perhaps a little inclined
to monopolize the discussion—a little intolerant of
opposition; yet if he assumed these as his privileges,
there was no man to whom we could more readily or
profitably grant them. For his discourse was truly in-
structive, engaging, at times eloquent. He seldom
attempted oratory, which perhaps he might have done
successfully. But he afforded a happy example of the
power of conversation to influence the minds of others,

whether of private friends and neighbors, or distinguished
public men.   With a mind naturally quick and compre-
hensive, he combined a memory which we may style
photographic; that is, retaining every impression it
received from the light of knowledge.   His leisure and
retirement afforded him ample time for reading.   Books,
journals, and periodicals were his constant companions,
and his political library was literally devoured to the
bone.   Few men could have been better schooled in the
political history of our country.

The precepts of Jefferson, Jackson, Madison, Hamilton, and a multitude of other statesmen of all parties,
were his, almost by heart.   And the fundamental principles of our institutions, the language of state papers,
documents, and constitutions, were to him as household
words.   He liked others, also, who were good talkers, or
at least who could do something indicating some mind.
He had a thorough contempt for empty show without
merit, even to the adornment of the outer man.   As for
example, we once heard him say "he had no admiration
for ten dollars' worth of beaver on ten cents' worth of
brains."

Sometimes we have thought he had a dislike for the
extremes of dress and fashion, even among the gentler
sex; although with ladies, as with men, he was decidedly
popular.   His conversation was none the less entertaining upon the daily affairs of life; as he dispensed the
hospitalities of his table; as he talked to friends and
guests of the family; as he dealt out cheerful badinage to
the dames of the household, while they held opposing
opinions and basted sophistry with their own needles.
Everywhere there was a certain aptness of expression, a
steady flow of good sense with just enough of the spice
and salt to season a true man.

5

Those who knew Colonel Crain in his own house, and with his own family, can remember, but can never impart to others, the emotions of pleasure and gratitude that filled their hearts. No reproduction can be made of the scene and the surroundings, no *résumé* of his reviving discourse, save to the eye and ear of memory.

William C. Crain died on the 16th of March, 1865. His five surviving children are Mrs. Henry J. Bowers of Cooperstown, the Hon. D. Jones Crain of New York, Mrs. John E. Warren of Chicago, R. T. Crain, Esq,. of the same place, and Dr. William B. Crain of Richfield Springs. His sister, Mrs. Baker, a widow of the late Hon. William Baker, resides at Utica, in this State.

G. R. T. HEWES.

THE oldest citizen that ever lived and died in the town of Richfield, was George Robert Twelve Hewes, who was born in the city of Boston, Nov. 5th, 1731. Mr. Lossing, in his History of the Revolution, says of Mr. Hewes :

" His early opportunities for acquiring education were very small. To Mrs. Tinkum, wife of the town-crier, he was indebted for his knowledge of reading and writing. Farming, fishing, and shoemaking seem to have been the chief employment of his earlier years. In 1758 he attempted to enlist in the army to serve against the French, but did not " pass muster ; " he was equally unsuccessful in attempts to join the navy, and then resumed shoemaking. In the various disturbances in Boston from the time of the passage of the Stamp Act, Hewes, who was both excitable and patriotic, was generally concerned. He was among the foremost in the destruction of the tea at Boston. Disguised as Indians, fifteen or twenty in number, they boarded several ships, and so vigorously did these men ply themselves, that within the space of three hours, three hundred and forty-two chests of tea were broken up, and their contents thrown into the dock. When the Americans invested the city, and many patriots were shut up under the vigilant eyes of the British officers, Hewes was among them. He managed to escape, and entered the naval service of the colonies as a privateer, in which he was somewhat successful. Afterwards he joined the army, and was stationed for a time at West Point, under General McDougal. He was never in any land battle, except with the Cow Boys and Skinners, as they were called, of the neutral ground of West Chester.

"After the Revolution he returned to Boston, and again engaged in business upon the sea.

"He, like Kinneson, was one of the thousands of that time utterly unknown to the world, except within the small love-circle of family relationship and neighborly regard; and even this present slight embalming of their memory would not have occurred, had not the contingency of great longevity distinguished them from other men. Although personally unknown, their deeds are felt in the political blessings we enjoy. * * * Returning to the residence of his son, G. R. T. Hewes, Jr., at Richfield, Otsego County, N. Y., he soon went down to the grave."

His son, G. R. T. Hewes, Jr., was for many years a resident of this place, and lived in a house that stood nearly opposite the present school-house in the western part of this village. This house was long since removed.

Old Mr. Hewes died Nov. 5th, 1840, aged one hundred and nine years and two months, as can now be seen on his tombstone in the church-yard.

HON. JONAS CLELAND.

JONAS CLELAND was a native of Massacnusetts, and was born in 1780. His father, Samuel Cleland, emigrated to the State of New York, and settled in the town of Warren, Herkimer County, in 1788, with his family, consisting of Norman, Salmon, Jonas, the subject of our sketch, Martin, and Moses.

Norman died in 1831, aged sixty-two. Salmon went to his final rest at the advanced age of eighty-four. Martin died when about twenty years old, and Moses still survives.* They were the first New England family that settled in the town of Warren. They lived first on the farm now occupied by Martin Goes, a short distance east of Richfield Springs, where they remained about one year, when they removed to Jordonville. Near the ruins of a house in Henderson, that had been destroyed by the Indians, they found the bleached bones of a man, which they buried, supposed to have been those of a Mr. Bell—one of the seven families that settled in Henderson prior to the Revolutionary War.

The republic being then in its infancy, disruptive forces were yet active ; and new institutions were encountering the difficulties of a recent formation. Born at such a period, the necessities of the day and peculiar exigencies of the times were well calculated to develop in the ambitious a spirit of self-reliance and force of character that so distinguished young Cleland.

The scarcity and defectiveness of educational institutions, left him very much to his own efforts to acquire knowledge, and a fitness for future usefulness and success. The degree of energy and determination with

* Since died.

which he encountered these early disadvantages, is best seen in the light of his long and honorable career. Perceiving that he must be the architect of his own fortune, he went manfully to work, acquired a good education, and was noted for industry and perseverence in every laudable undertaking ; thus establishing a character that entitled him to the confidence of the public.

On reaching his majority, he was at once admitted to the seat of magistracy in Herkimer County, which office he held for forty years in succession, during which time he never had a suit reversed. He was elected a member of the State Legislature in 1814, and held the office several terms ; was an ardent supporter of the Erie Canal project, then in agitation. In one of his speeches in support of this canal, he made this prediction: " that before 1875, tea from China and Japan would come to New York by way of the Pacific Ocean, the great lakes, and the Erie Canal." Previous to the formation of the Republican party he was a Democrat of the old school, but in 1856 was a firm supporter of the Republican platform, and his affiliations continued with this party through the remainder of his life. He represented his town in the Board of Supervisors for several years ; was also judge of the Court of Common Pleas of Herkimer County. While acting as judge, Nathaniel Foster, the renowned hunter and trapper of Northern New York, was tried for shooting Peter Waters, a St. Regis Indian, in the spring of 1834.

The Hon. Hiram Denio, the circuit judge, presided, assisted by Jonas Cleland, John B. Dygert, Abijah Osborn, and Richard Henderson, judges of the Common Pleas. During the trial, the prisoner's counsel asked one of the witnesses on the stand if he heard this Indian threaten the life of Foster. Objection being made,

Judge Denio sustained the objection, and ruled that such evidence was not admissible, without consulting the other judges. Judge Cleland dissented from the decision, and was sustained by two of the other judges, thus over-ruling the decision of the presiding judge.

He was also agent of the Henderson and Douglas estate, and superintended the erection of the mansion called the "Henderson Home."

He was twice married, first to Lydia Talcott, in 1805, who lived but two years, and again in 1818 to Abigail Tisdale, of Connecticut, by whom he had two sons and one daughter.

Judge Cleland died on Sunday, April 25th, 1858, aged seventy-eight years; was confirmed by Bishop Wain-wright, August 5th, 1853. A short time previous to his death, although apparently in his usual health, he called his youngest son to his side, saying, "This is the last day that I shall be with you in this tabernacle of clay. It is my request that you go to Richfield Springs, and ascertain the condition of John W. Tunnicliff" (Mr. Tunnicliff was very ill at this time), who was a relative by marriage. They were both members of the Episcopal Church.

On learning that Mr. Tunnicliff was not expected to live, he said, "I shall cross the river first, and be there to welcome him home." He then wrote a farewell letter to his son at Frankfort; sent for Mr. Hyde, the undertaker, and gave full directions in relation to his funeral; ordered the suit brought into the room, that was to clothe his remains after death; wrote in his Prayer Book the names of those he wished to bear him to his final resting-place; sank back in his chair, in the full possession of all his faculties, and quietly ceased to breathe. The death of such men fills the heart of all with inexpressible sadness, and leaves a vacancy, that time alone can obliterate.

Judge Cleland was kind, courteous, and charitable to all, and his many private virtues will long be remembered by those who knew him.

His daughter, Lydia, wife of the late. Prof. John Abbott, now resides with her son, George C. Abbott, in Michigan.

E. T. Cleland, the eldest son, was an attorney, and resided at Frankfort. Was clerk of Herkimer County one term. He died in 1861, leaving one son, Charles B. Cleland.

George M. Cleland, the youngest son, now resides on the old homestead of his father in Jordonville. Has filled various offices in his town and county. Was elected sheriff in 1864, and was, previous to that time, supervisor and justice of the peace of the town of Warren. Was again elected to the said offices, his term expiring the present year. He still uses the same "desk" and office room that his worthy father used during the protracted period of his official life.

HON. JAMES HYDE.

PROMINENT in the list of distinguished men of Otsego County, stands the name of the Hon. James Hyde, of the town of Richfield. Through a long line of renowned ancestry, he was born at Franklin, Connecticut, May 26th, 1797. (*Chancellor Walworth's Genealogy of the Hyde Family*, vol. i.) His father removed to Richfield in the year 1800, and held various local offices in the town, and twice represented the County of Otsego in the State Legislature. He died in 1826.

The subject of this sketch was but a child when his parents removed to this new section, surrounded by primitive forests, far from the privileges of high schools and other facilities of education. But he early manifested a desire for books, and eagerly pursued the various branches of an English education. Surrounded by the hallowed and priceless influences of Christian parents and associates, through childhood and youth he was ever exempt from the vices and moral pollutions that so generally vitiate the youth of the present day. While yet in his minority he left the paternal roof, and for several years was engaged as merchants' clerk in the city of Buffalo. Accurate and prompt in business, and ambitious for knowledge, his spare hours were occupied in the use of books, whose charms were augmented by their perusal. He longed for greater privileges of education than he had ever enjoyed; but this was never granted, and became a source of deep regret in later years. But few ever attain to the degree of proficiency that he possessed under similar circumstances, the legitimate fruits of a determined spirit whose resolutions overcame all obstacles in their progress. The higher branches were at length attained, and his youthful days were occupied in the investigation of the sciences, and in the study of nature and gaining the elements of philosophical knowledge from her original economy and laws. In the year 1818, having reached his majority, he returned to Richfield, and immediately engaged in the mercantile trade, which, however, was pursued but a short period of time. Inspired with a restless ambition for preferment, his attention was directed to the study of law, and the works of Blackstone, Cowen, and other eminent jurists were the constant companions of his leisure hours while in trade; and subsequently his time was given exclusively to reading in the leading law-offices of the county seat. In 1831, he was duly admitted to practice, and opened an office at Richfield Springs, where he at once received a successful patronage. At the age of twenty-five he was married to Miss Fanny Beardsley, daughter of Obadiah Beardsley, of this town, and sister of Judges Levi and Samuel Beardsley of Utica. As previously noticed, she is at present the only surviving member of her father's family.

In 1820 he was initiated into the mysteries of "Free Masonry," and was ever a steadfast adherent and advocate of this ancient and honorable institution, notwithstanding the violent persecutions that arose in 1828, from the mysterious disappearance of William Morgan, whose fate was unjustly attributed to the relentless rigor of the laws that were supposed to govern this secret organization. The history of this persecution is familiar to every intelligent reader. It is sufficient to know that this ancient order had its origin at the building of the Holy Temple of Jerusalem, and has been perpetuated through the divine dispensation to the present day, and still claims the respect of the civilized world. And not only so, but eminent and distinguished men of all Christian nations have been and are still established patrons of the order.

James Hyde was an ardent admirer of Masonry, embracing as it does the liberal arts and sciences, and is in truth the great auxiliary of the Christian church. He was master of the lodge at Richfield Springs for many years, and was also one of the Grand Wardens of the Grand Lodge of Masons of the State of New York. His first votes were given to the Democratic party. Previous to the campaign of 1828, he had taken no very active position in the political field. He was an ardent supporter of General Jackson, and the platform on which he was elected President of the United States, in 1828.

Under his administration, he was appointed the first

postmaster of Richfield Springs, then known as East Richfield. He held this office for more than twelve years; and until the accession of the Whig party to power, under General Harrison, when he resigned.

He was captain and lieutenant-colonel of artillery in the State militia, his commission being signed by DeWitt Clinton, then Governor of the State. He was appointed master in chancery by William L. Marcy, was removed by Governor Seward, and reappointed by Governor Bouck, retaining the office until its abolishment, by the adoption of the State Constitution, in 1847. In May of that year, he was elected judge of Otsego County, holding his position until January, 1852.

He served as justice of the peace, at different times, comprising a period of more than thirty years. At the time of the formation of the Republican party in 1855 he unreservedly embraced its principles, and was one of its leading advocates the remainder of his life.

He was ever regarded as a man of strict integrity and honor, and his decisions in courts of justice were usually regarded as final. A man of exalted liberality in every good work, he was in spirit and in truth a consistent Christian philanthropist. It is true he was not above all the prejudices and influences of education, but his was one of those pure, beneficent spirits, which from their nature belong to the whole of mankind. He was indeed a noble example of exalted virtue, with a soul inspired with fraternal ardor for the best interests of those by whom he was surrounded. Judge Hyde was a man of more than ordinary ability, especially as an eminent counsellor in the realm of jurisprudence. In a brief sketch of men of this class, it is extremely difficult to present a just view of the many private virtues that adorn their general character. "With a hand open as day

for melting charity," the poor always found in Judge
Hyde a true friend, ever ready to bestow on the unfortunate and afflicted, his generosity being measured only
by his means.

He did not submit to commands because the Law-
giver was powerful and could punish disobedience, nor
yet simply because He was just and His commands equit-
able ; but his spirit voluntarily went forth to co-operate
in all the designs of goodness, with a pure Christian
motive. He loved God, not merely as his great benefac-
tor, but as the only source of hope and felicity to all sentient, rational existence.

He loved mankind, not only because they were of
the same race as himself, but because they were susceptible of virtue and happiness in this life, and heirs of an
eternal inheritance in the future state. This putting
forth of the affections from and above himself, was his
ennobling and distinctive characteristic. He was a liberal supporter of the Presbyterian Church at Richfield
Springs, and was a regular attendant upon its services.
He died May 1st, 1862.

He sleeps in the village church-yard beneath a plain
marble monument, overshadowed by the lofty branches
of vigorous maples planted by his own hand, and that
now guard the last resting-place of the honored *dead*.

The following tribute to his memory was furnished
by a talented lady friend in New York,* who is a regular contributor to several leading magazines :

> When the soft sigh of September
> Stirs each bough of gleaming gold,
> Then the maple-trees remember
> That beneath the grassy mould

* Ethel Lynn.

Lies the hand which set them thither
  Slender saplings long ago ;
And their leaves like tear-drops tender
  Lightly fall and rest below.
There a spirit's mortal robing
  Lies where dear familiar feet
Linger lovingly about it,
  Tread each day the shadowed street.
There low voices hushed and softly
  Tell of good deeds shyly done—
Of an honored life unsullied—
  Of a crown untarnished won—
Of the mystic tie unbroken—
  Of the hand no bribe could soil—
Active brain forever busy
  Wrong to right and craft to foil ;—
Whisper of the mansion ready,
  With its pearly door ajar,
With the Master's mark upon it—
  A footstep roughened by a scar.
Then drop above him, kindly *Autumn*,
  Ruddy, flushed, and golden leaves :
When a good man goes up higher
  Only tender heart-blood grieves—
Weave no pall to lie above him,
  But a glory like the sun,
Or a conqueror's robe of triumph
  When the fight at last is won.

WHEELER PALMER, M. D.,

Son of Christopher Palmer, was born in Colchester, Connecticut, in 1791. While still a child his parents emigrated to the State of New York, and settled in the town of Exeter, Otsego County.

At the age of nineteen he commenced the study of medicine with Dr. John B. Elwood, of Warren, afterwards with Dr. Seldin Graves, of Richfield, and subse-

Wheeler Palmer

quently with Dr. Joseph White, of Cherry Valley, comprising a period of three years ; and graduated with the highest honors of the censors of the Otsego County Medical Society at Cooperstown, in May, 1817, Joseph White being president of the society. He immediately commenced the practice of medicine and surgery in company with Dr. Graves, of Brighton, his former preceptor ; and at the expiration of six months bought out the entire interest of his partner, and continued a successful and growing practice alone. Relying entirely upon his own resources, without the adventitious aids of fortune, he soon found himself the master of an extensive field of usefulness in the medical profession. In March, 1818, he was married to a *Miss Brown*, of Plainfield, who died in 1832, leaving two sons. In 1834, he was again married to Mrs. Hartwell, of Richfield Springs, who died in October, 1858.

When Dr. Palmer was a boy about sixteen years of age, while driving a yoke of oxen for his father, accidentally one of them stepped on his foot, but nothing serious was apprehended from the slight injury, although it remained painful at times ; but a small tumor finally appeared. He at once consulted Dr. Delos White and other distinguished surgeons, with a view to its removal ; but nothing was done, and it continued many years without material change. At length it began to enlarge and became extremely painful, bleeding profusely at times. In October, 1859, he went to Albany, where it was operated upon by Dr. March, at the medical college ; but inflammation supervened, followed by typhoid fever, which terminated fatally, January 5th, 1860.

His remains were buried at Richfield Springs. In the death of Dr. Palmer, the medical profession lost one of its most worthy and honored members ; the church a consistent and devoted Christian, the community in which he lived a beloved, worthy citizen and eminent physician, whose tender sympathy in their hours of affliction, will long be remembered by many families in this vicinity, who cherish his memory with the most sincere affection and esteem.

JOHN GANO

WAS a native of France, and emigrated to the United States and settled in New Jersey a short time previous to the Revolutionary War. He removed with his family to the town of Richfield, in 1791, and, in company with James Williamson,* purchased six hundred acres of land in Schuyler's patent, lot No. 8. Mr. Gano built a log-cabin near the site of the present residence of Mr. Allison Orendorf, where he continued to reside until his death, leaving three sons and three daughters. James, the eldest son, was the father of James H. and Benjamin Gano, who are now residents of this village. James H. Gano now owns and occupies a portion of the land that was embraced in the original purchase of his grandfather in 1791.

JOSEPH LAYTON

WAS born in New Jersey, February 26th, 1774. Removed with his parents when a child to Hoosick, N. Y. Remembered the battle of Bennington, that was fought on his father's farm.

Emigrated to Richfield in 1795, where he purchased a farm of 210 acres on the west bank of Canadarago Lake,

---

* Grandfather of Cyrus Williamson, of the town of Warren.

where he continued to reside until his death, June 12th, 1859. Had four children; two now living. Harvey Layton now owns and occupies the original estate of his father.

JOHN GARRET

Was a passenger on the vessel with John Tunnicliff. He purchased a tract of land in the valley of the Butternut Creek, and was the founder of Garretsville, Otsego County, N. Y.

Mr. Garret and wife were taken prisoners by the Indians, during the Revolution, and were absent from their home seven years.

At the time of their capture, as they saw the Indians approaching their cabin, Mrs. Garret, seizing her clock and silver-ware, fled out of the back door, concealing the silver under an inverted pig-trough, and the clock was thrown hastily under the garden fence, where they were found on their return from captivity.

GERSHON SKINNER.

Gershon Skinner * was a Revolutionary soldier, and lived at Little Falls. Held the commission of adjutant in the army. Was a miller by trade, and occupied a large stone mill at the above place, in 1778. This mill was a place of refuge during the war for women and children, and served also as a fort. In the autumn of

---

* Grandfather of Mr. John Skinner, of the town of Columbia, who has now in his possession a *trunk* and *pocket-book*, rescued from the burning *mill*, the property of his grandfather.

1778, it was attacked by about 500 Indians and Tories, who finally succeeded in overcoming the feeble garrison, killing three men, and taking prisoners the helpless women and children, about forty in number, who were soon after released, and returned to their homes. After a severe hand-to-hand conflict with four savages, Mr. Skinner succeeded in making his escape by plunging into a dark recess, in the lower part of the mill, where he remained nearly under water, until driven out by the flames of the burning building over his head.

Mr. Skinner died in Columbia in 1824, at an advanced age.

JOHN RUSSELL.

Among the number of passengers who came to this country from England on board the ship with Mr. Tunnicliff in 1758, were John Russell and George Johnson, who were at this time young men. John Russell was a carpenter by trade, and was employed at once by Mr. Tunnicliff at the " Oaks." A dwelling was erected, previous to the building of a saw-mill, and the lumber for the house was all sawed by Mr. Russell, with a "*whip saw.*" He continued in the service of Mr. Tunnicliff three years, receiving one acre of land for each day's work. The land thus purchased is located in the extreme western part of the town of Otsego, on the " *Otego* " Creek, originally embracing 900 acres, on which John Russell continued to reside until his *death*, in 1832, leaving eight children. Two of his sons, William and Thomas, occupied the original land of their father's purchase, until their death. William Russell died March 16th, 1859, aged seventy-two years three months and ten days. Thomas Russell died December 5th, 1857, aged fifty-eight years.

GEORGE JOHNSON

PURCHASED a tract of land near Oaksville, about four miles south of Canadarago Lake, where he erected the mills now owned by P. E. Johnson, a grandson.

DEACON JONATHAN BLOOMFIELD

EMIGRATED from New Jersey in 1790, and settled near this village, in the town of Warren, Herkimer County. Here he purchased a farm of 120 acres, of Mr. Hull Thomas.* Two of his sons, Samuel and Joseph, continued to ocupy this farm until their death, it having been divided between these brothers. Soon after his settlement, Jonathan Bloomfield built the saw-mill on Ocquionis Creek, known as the Bloomfield Mill. While the dam for this mill was being constructed, Mr. Bloomfield sent his son Joseph (a lad only nine years of age) into the adjacent forest with his hatchet to cut brush to be used in the construction of the dam.

He had been at work but a short time, however, when he was startled by a huge black bear, slowly approaching, but a short distance away. He immediately fled to the mill, breathless with fear, where he related the adventure, and his narrow escape. Joseph Bloomfield died July 26th, 1862, aged seventy-two years, leaving one son, Mr. Allen Bloomfield,† who is now a *resident* of this village.

---

* Descendants of Mr. Thomas are now residents of the town of Winfield.

† David C. Bloomfield, a younger brother of Allen Bloomfield, was accidentally shot while out sporting in the woods on his father's farm, in the summer of 1854. He was twenty-eight years of age.

Deacon Samuel Bloomfield inherited that portion of his father's estate including the "*Mill.*" He died December 23d, 1866, aged eighty-two years and four months, leaving two sons and *three* daughters. Mr. Bloomfield was an exemplary member and officer of the Presbyterian Church of this village for many years.

RICHARD SCHOOLEY

WAS among the first settlers of the town of Warren, where he purchased a farm, about two miles north of Richfield Springs. He had eleven children, of whom but one son (Wm. Schooley, Esq.) and three daughters are now living.

Soon after his settlement here, an incident occurred, worthy of notice. The forests at this time were full of wild animals, who frequently trespassed upon the cultivated fields of the settlers. On one occasion, two of Mr. Schooley's sons, John and Henry, lads of thirteen and fifteen *years*, discovered that their father's corn-field had been ravaged by some native of the forest. They determined to watch for the intruder, and, if possible, ascertain its true character. At sun-down the following evening, preparing themselves with their father's gun heavily loaded, and some pieces of boards for a seat, they proceeded to the corn-field, and located themselves in the top of a wide-spreading beech-tree that stood on the border of the field. Here they awaited the approach of the trespasser. The night was dark, and nothing disturbed the stillness of the hours but the monotonous hum of insect life. About ten o'clock they heard the crackling of brush in the edge of the neighboring forest, and the hoarse snuffing of some large animal, as it approached the corn-field. Peering through the thick darkness, they indistinctly discerned some dark object slowly moving among the corn. Deliberately pointing the gun in the direction of the object, they fired; a brief rustling noise followed, and all was again silent. With emotions of trepidation, they cautiously descended the tree, and fled to their father's house. Here they procured a *lantern*, and arming themselves with *pitch-forks*, returned to the corn-field, where they found the lifeless body of a large black bear, which they dragged in triumph to their home.

Richard Schooley died in December, 1853, aged ninty-five years.

THOMAS FREEMAN

Was born in 1791. Emigrated to the town of Warren in 1807, and still resides where he first settled, near the village. Is a mason by trade.

THE MASON FAMILY.

Sampson Mason (American root of this family) was a dragoon in Oliver Cromwell's army, and supposed to belong to his "*troop*," at the battle of "*Marston Moor*," in 1644. The precise date of his arrival in this country, and settlement in Dorchester, Suffolk County, Mass., is unknown. A "*will*," executed by him July 25th, 1649, and on record in the above county, makes his settlement anterior to this date.

He had thirteen children. Died Sept. 15th, 1676, at

an advanced age. Six of his sons reached the age of from seventy to ninty-four years.

Isaac Mason,* a lineal descendant, settled in the town of Warren, Herkimer County, N. Y., on lands adjoining the Cruger estate, on the north, in 1804. His youngest son, James Mason, is now a resident of this *village.*

JOHN BATES

EMIGRATED from Sharon, Connecticut, in 1830, and settled on the east shore of Canadarago Lake, where he purchased three hundred acres of land, on which he continued to reside until his death, September 18th, 1856, leaving five sons and three daughters.

This rich and highly cultivated estate, now in possession of two of his sons, is regarded as one of the finest farms in this part of the State. The Bates brothers are noted as extensive stock-raisers, and dealers in the best qualities of imported cattle.

TUNIS VROMAN

WAS a native of Schoharie County, N. Y. At the age of ten years, in 1776, in company with three of his brothers, he was made prisoner by the Indians and taken to Canada. While on the way, a younger brother cried to return home, was taken to one side by a Tory, his throat cut, and his body thrown over a log, where it was left. The writer heard Mr. Vroman relate this circumstance. His parents were both killed by the Indians near their

---

* Isaac Mason died July 18th, 1866, aged eighty-nine years four months and twenty-seven days.

residence. The mother was struck on the head several times with a tomahawk, before she fell. Tunis was kept a prisoner one year and returned to his friends. He subsequently removed to the town of Warren, Herkimer County, then to Columbia, and died in July, 1866, aged one hundred years, leaving two sons and four daughters. One son* and three daughters are now living.

HON. OLCOTT C. CHAMBERLAIN

Was born in Colchester, Connecticut, November 12th, 1793; removed with his father's family to this town, where they arrived July 6th, 1797, and settled on a farm when it was a wilderness, and on which he resided until his death.

He was one of the earliest members of our County Agricultural Society, and gave it his earnest and undivided support, and for a time was Vice-President of the State Agricultural Society. In the years 1841 and 1848 was one of the Representatives of this county in the Assembly. Mr. Chamberlain was married in 1813, to Miss Cornelia Tunnicliff,† by whom he had four sons and two daughters. He died in 1860, aged sixty-seven years.

HON. ALFORD CHAMBERLAIN,

Son of Olcott C. Chamberlain, was born at Richfield Springs, April 10th, 1821. In 1847 he was married to a daughter of Dr. Ransom, of Camden, Oneida County, and

* Peter Vroman, Esq., of South Columbia.

† Daughter of William Tunnicliff, the first settler of Richfield Springs.

became a resident of that place. Was elected supervisor
of the town of Camden. Received the appointment of
under-sheriff, which office he held about five years.
Returned to the town of Richfield in 1860, was elected
member of Assembly in 1871, and re-elected in 1872.
He died October 18th, 1872, leaving one son to inherit
his large estate.

GIDEON WILBUR.

GIDEON WILBUR was born in Rhode Island, April 9th,
1766. Was left an orphan when but a lad. Was
bound out to learn the carpenter's trade, which he followed until 1786, when he was married, and came to
Dutchess County, N. Y., where he bought a farm and
remained until 1804, when he emigrated with his family
to Warren, Herkimer County, and purchased a farm, on
which he lived to see seven sons and four daughters
grow up, become married, and settled. He died July
6th, 1862, aged ninety-six years.

Mr. Wilbur was remarkably active to the last year
of his life. Of the seven sons, but one now survives.
The late Mr. Eseck Wilbur, of the town of Warren, was
a son of Gideon Wilbur.

EZEKIEL COMSTOCK

WAS born at New London, Connecticut, February
16th, 1774. Removed with his father to Berkshire
County, Massachusetts, the summer before New London
was burned. Phoebe Comstock, his wife, was born at
Williamstown, Massachusetts, October 20th, 1776, and

was married at the above place, July 13th, 1798. They removed to Granville, Washington County, New York, in 1804, and to Warren, Herkimer County, in November 1832, thence to Richfield Springs in April, 1850. Jay L. Comstock, Esq., of this place, was their only son. Ezekiel Comstock died February 16th, 1866, aged ninety-two years. His wife, Phoebe Comstock, survived him nearly eight years, and died November 5th, 1873, aged ninety-seven years and sixteen days. Isaac Holmes, father of Mrs. Phoebe Comstock, was a soldier of the Revolution, and participated in the battle of Bennington, Vermont. He died in Warren in 1843, aged ninety-two years.

EDWARD CHEESEMAN.

Mr. Cheeseman was among the earliest settlers of this region. At an early day he kept a store at " Federal Corners," near this place, and subsequently removed to the village, where he discovered and manufactured the popular patent medicine known as " Cheeseman's Arabian Balsam." The great demand that followed the discovery of this article, resulted in a comfortable fortune for Mr. Cheeseman. He died August 13th, 1840, aged sixty-five years, leaving one son and two daughters. Mrs. Edward Cheeseman died August 18th, 1840. Their monument can now be seen in the old cemetery near the Presbyterian church.

" Cheeseman's Arabian Balsam " is now manufactured in Brooklyn by E. B. Green, grandson of Mr. Cheeseman.

DARIUS H. CARY,

Son of Joseph Cary, came to the town of Richfield from Coventry, Rhode Island, in the year 1800, in company with Ephraim Carr, who settled in the town of Hartwick, Otsego County. Mr. Cary was a carpenter by trade; was married to Miss Patty Whitney, of Brooklyn, Connecticut. He received a captain's commission of a company of cavalry of the Eleventh Regiment of New York. Said commission was signed by Daniel D. Tompkins, Governor, May 23d, 1814. Captain Cary worked at his trade until he was forty years old ; he then bought a farm near Monticello, on which he continued to reside until his death, February 8th, 1868, aged ninety-one years. Mr. Edwin Cary, his only son, is now a resident of Saquoit, Oneida County.

ISAAC DE LONG

Was born in Dutchess County, New York, in 1771, and when a lad removed to Columbia County, where at the age of nineteen he married Rebecca Allen, aged fifteen years. In 1795 they removed to the town of Warren, Herkimer County, where they commenced life with comparatively nothing. A farm was now purchased, and after years of untiring industry was paid for. Another farm adjoining was subsequently purchased, and from this time forward it was comparatively easy for them to add to their possessions. They reared a family of nine children, five sons and four daughters. The second son, named George, was killed by the falling of a tree when eleven years of age. The youngest of the nine, a son, whom they also called George, was killed at the age of twenty-two, by being thrown from a horse. At the present time there are but two of the family living, namely, Charles,* who was elected a member of the State Legislature in 1852, from Herkimer County, and Isaac Jr., now a resident of this village.

Isaac De Long died in 1858, aged eighty-seven years, and his wife died in 1865, aged ninety years, both highly respected by all who knew them.

ELIAS BRAMAN

CAME to the town of Richfield previous to the last war with England, and purchased a farm of one hundred acres, about one mile to the west of this village. This farm was subsequently enlarged by additional purchases, until it finally embraced 290 acres. Mr. Braman constructed the section of the Great Western turnpike that passed through the town of Richfield. Also built the cotton factory at Van-Hornsville, and the stone gristmill near the covered bridge on his estate. He died † March 14, 1845, aged sixty-six years, leaving a large fortune to his only son, Elias Braman, Jr., who, in 1846, erected the present substantial mansion now owned and occupied by Mr. Peter Bush.

* Hon. Charles De Long, now a resident of Peoria, Illinois.

† During his life, Mr. Braman ordered a limestone " sarcophagus " cut and prepared to receive his remains after death, in which his burial-case was placed in the ground.

AUGUSTUS H. WARD.

MR. WARD and family commenced visiting this place
in the year 1851, as guests at the American Hotel. In
the year 1853, he purchased the *Benedict* Cottage. This
cottage occupied a most delightful location on the north
side of Main Street, standing in the midst of a beautiful grove of ornamental trees and shrubbery, and
bounded on the north by Lake Clement. Mr. Ward
subsequently made extensive purchases of real estate
here, which he greatly improved, adding much to the
beauty and ornamentation of the village, and enhancing
the value of all other property in the place. He was a
man of enlarged views and generous impulses. To
every appeal for aid in public improvements, as well as
for every other worthy object, he was open-handed.
He continued to occupy his cottage * here with his family, annually through the summer season, till the time
of his death, in February, 1868. He donated to the Episcopal church the grounds for the rectory, and contributed liberally toward the completion and support of
the church.

In 1872, his only son, E. A. Ward, erected an English cottage on James Street, where he now resides.

GENERAL WILLIAM P. JOHNSON

WAS born near Oaksville, Otsego County, December
31st, 1810. His grandfather, George Johnson, came to
this country from England in 1758, on board the vessel

---

* This cottage was accidentally burned in July, 1868.

with John Tunnicliff, and located on the Oaks Creek, immediately after the Revolution. He built the mills at what is now known as Cat-town near Oaksville. These mills with adjoining lands were afterwards inherited by William P. Johnson and his brothers. William P. Johnston was a merchant at this place for a number of years, and finally purchased the American Hotel at Richfield Springs, in 1839, and remained its successful proprietor until his death, June 21st, 1871, leaving his large property to his widow and four daughters.

WILLIAM G. MOORE,

Son of James Moore, was born in Woodbridge, New Jersey, August 11th, 1801. Emigrated with his parents to Herkimer County, in 1803. Mr. Moore says, "My parents, with their seven children, embarked on board a sloop on Staten Island Sound, and sailed up the Hudson River to Albany. From the latter point we were conveyed by wagon, with all our effects, through the wilderness to 'Freeman's Mills,' in the town of Warren." Mr. Moore became a resident of Richfield Springs, in 1829. Has been a popular horse-trainer more than fifty-three years. Is the only member of his father's family now living.

DANIEL HARRINGTON

Was born in the town of Mansfield, Windham County, Conn., August 13th, 1795. Removed to Winfield, Herkimer County, N. Y., in 1810, where he continued to reside until 1861, when he removed to the town of Richfield, and now resides in this village with his son, Mr. DeWitt Harrington.

JAMES ROY, JR.

In the month of September, 1869, a sad casualty occurred on Canadarago Lake. James Roy, Jr., only son of Mr. James Roy, of West Troy, N. Y., left the dock at the Lake House alone in a row-boat, for the purpose of bathing. Was last seen rowing across the lake. In about two hours after, the boat, containing his apparel, was found floating against the western shore. Search was at once made for his body, but without avail until the ninth day, when it was found floating on the surface directly over the Sunken Island. It was taken in charge by his father, and conveyed to Troy for interment.

LINES BY ETHEL LYNN

All day upon the rippled lake
  Dark rushes write the story,
All night the moon tells tenderly
  Of youth gone up to glory.

Red sunset waves sing soberly
  The kiss they softly gave him ;
The last pale lily murmurs yet
  She saw, but could not save him.

O angel mother ! from above
  Sawest thou the white soul only,
Nor through the stars watched all the night
  The wave-washed body lonely ?

I know not ; only this I know,
  Nor sea, nor lake, nor river
Shall threaten more the lad at rest,
  Ashore with thee forever.

AUGUSTUS R. ELWOOD.

(From Life Sketches of Members of the Legislature, 1870, by Boone and Cook.)

Hon. A. R. Elwood is the successor of Mr. Van Petten, and represents the Twentieth Senatorial District, comprising the counties of Herkimer and Otsego. He was born at Richfield Springs, Otsego County, October 18th, 1819, where he still resides. He is of English and German descent upon his father's side. His maternal ancestors came from Connecticut. His family were old settlers of Otsego, and its members have been among its most staunch residents. His father was an industrious and successful farmer.

Mr. Elwood commenced life as a merchant, in which pursuit, by his active business habits, his resolute will, and exemplary character, he won the confidence and esteem of his fellow-citizens. Owing to ill health, he withdrew from personal participation in mercantile pursuits a few years since, although still retaining his interest in the establishment. Mr. Elwood, even before he came of age, took a warm interest in politics. In early life he was a Democrat, and contributed largely to the success of that party in his section. He was appointed postmaster of Richfield Springs in 1842, and held the office until 1848. He was also deputy sheriff of the county in 1841. In the controversies of the period, within the Democratic ranks, Mr. Elwood zealously supported Free-soil principles. He was a member of the famous Buffalo Convention, and has ever remained a consistent and zealous exponent of its cardinal ideas. He supported Martin Van Buren for President in 1848, for which offence he was removed from the office of postmaster by President Polk, whom he had helped to elect. Mr. Elwood's political tact, discerning judgment, organizing talent, and ability to shrewdly forecast events, led the people frequently to send him to the conventions of his party; and he has thus taken a prominent part in the initiative of many important public movements. He was a member of the convention held at Saratoga Springs in 1855, and assisted in the organization of the National Republican party in Philadelphia, in 1856, voting for the nomination of John C. Fremont. He was also a delegate to the Chicago Convention in 1860, casting his vote for Abraham Lincoln. In 1862 and 1863 he was Chairman of the Republican County Committee, in which capacity he exhibited marked sagacity and resources as a party manager.

Mr. Elwood is very popular in his native county, notwithstanding the Republican party there, unfortunately for itself, has been fearfully torn by warring factions. He held the office of county clerk during the term beginning in 1859 and expiring in 1861, and was supervisor of his town from 1865 to 1868, and for two years served as chairman of the Board. Efforts have been frequently made to induce him to allow the use of his name for various honorable positions, but he has uniformly declined. During the late political campaign, Mr. Elwood contested for the nomination of the Republican Convention with Hon. William W. Campbell, formerly justice of the Supreme Court and member of Assembly in 1869. The canvass was a brisk one, resulting in the nomination and triumphant election of the former. Mr. Elwood is not a debater in the ordinary acceptation of the term, although, when occasion demands, he expresses his views with great clearness and cogency. He has also those higher qualifications necessary to a successful legislator, and which are peculiar to organizing and executive minds. Mr. Elwood, in 1846, married a daughter of the late Hon. James Hyde, an estimable and educated lady, whose occasional contributions to the literature of the day display marked originality of conception, deep thought, and beauty of diction. Mr. Elwood is of medium stature and slender build, but of that wiry and nervous organization which but needs a moderate degree of health to accomplish great results.

HON. BENJAMIN PRINGLE *

Was born November 9th, 1807, in the town of Richfield, Otsego County, New York, and is a descendant of the Pringles of Scotland, a numerous, distinguished, and ancient family. His father was one of the pioneers of Otsego County, and instrumental in organizing the present school system of the State. Mr. Pringle received his education at the common school, academy, and under private tutors. He then engaged in the study of the law, and having been admitted to the bar, entered into a co-partnership with Hon. Heman J. Redfield at Batavia, Genesee County. At a later period he was elected judge and president of the Genesee Bank, and took a prominent part in the "Holland Land Company." He was elected senator in the Thirty-third and Thirty-fourth Congresses, where he held the position of chairman of the Committee of Indian Affairs. The following year he was elected member of the Legislature, and in 1863 was appointed by President Lincoln judge of the Court of Justice established at Cape Town, South Africa, under the treaty between America and Great Britain for the sup-

* Albany Times, March, 1873.

pression of the African slave-trade, where he remained seven years. He has taken great interest in church matters, having been thrice appointed deputy from his diocese to the Triennial Convention of the Protestant Episcopal Church of the United States.

Judge Pringle is a tall and somewhat portly man, with a mild, benevolent, and intellectual countenance, broad, high forehead, white hair and moustache. He is modest and unassuming, and although taking a great interest in all the proceedings of the Constitutional Commission of which he is now a member (1873), he seldom is given to long speeches, but a few words of information, advice, or explanation from him at a fitting time, given in a low, placid tone, never fail to produce effect.

The parents of Judge Pringle resided, at the time of his birth, on the farm known as the Captain Cary estate, a short distance north of Monticello.

HUMPHREY PALMER, ESQ.

In addition to Dr. Manley, there are several others between eighty and ninety years of age, now residents of this village, that we propose to notice briefly.

HUMPHREY PALMER was four years of age when his parents emigrated from Colchester, Connecticut, in 1794, to a farm in the town of Exeter, Otsego County, about two miles west of the lake, on Herkimer Creek. Remembers distinctly the incidents of the journey through the wilderness. Was married in 1813. Has two sons and one daughter. Was drafted in 1812 to serve under Colonel Stranahan. Hired a substitute, who was killed in action. In 1834 he removed to this village, and was elected justice of the peace in 1840, and held the office five years. He had three brothers and three sisters, who were all living in 1870, the united ages of the seven aggregating 528 years; a remarkable instance of the longevity of an unbroken family.

JACOB WALTER

WAS born in Fort Plain,* Montgomery County, N. Y., February 14th, 1788. Remained with his father until May 3d, 1803, when he was bound apprentice to Joseph Farr, a watch and clock maker. The present village of Fort Plain at this time contained but one house. " The first settlement of Fort Plain was situated a short distance to the west, and was destroyed by the Indians during the Revolution." Mr. Walter says "a Presbyterian church stood on 'Sand Hill,' but was subsequently burned by lightning." After serving seven years to learn the trade, he continued in the employment of Mr. Farr two years, when he opened a shop on his own account at "Hall Settlement," in the town of Minden, in 1810. He continued here three years, and removed to the "Little Lakes," in the southern part of Herkimer County; but soon after located in the town of Springfield, where he remained twenty-seven years. In 1845 he established his business in the village of Richfield Springs, where he now resides at the age of eighty-six.

Mr. Walter was married in 1811, and has eight sons and one daughter now living.† Mr. P. D. Walter, the present mayor of the city of Lockport, N. Y., is a son of Jacob Walter. ‡

* His father, Christian Walter, was of German descent, a farmer, and his residence stood on the elevated ground near the old fort.

† Since writing the above, one son, Alonzo Walter, of Ingersoll, Canada West, has died.

‡ Jacob Walter has in his house at the present time a brass clock made by himself over " sixty years " ago, and which is now in good running order.

WILLIAM HAYES

Was born in Yardley Gubion, Northamptonshire, England, June 4th, 1791. Learned the trade of paper manufacturer, which he followed until 1832, when he emigrated to America, and settled in Sangerfield, Oneida County, as a farmer. Was married in 1816, and had one son, who died at Sangerfield in 1857, leaving a wife and seven children.

Mr. Hayes removed to this town in 1849, where he now resides.

JOHN FISH

Was born in Montgomery County, N. Y., December 10th, 1791. Was a carpenter by trade, and married in 1819. Had three sons and three daughters. His son, John D. Fish, enlisted in the summer of 1862 in the 121st Regiment New York Volunteers, then stationed at Mohawk; was soon after promoted to a captaincy, and while leading his men in action on the 12th of May, 1864, at Spottsylvania Court House, was shot dead by the enemy. Mr. Fish has been a resident of this village since 1826.

TIMOTHY GREEN

Was born in the town of Archfield, Massachusetts, February 3d, 1791. Emigrated to the town of Richfield, Otsego County, with his parents, in 1794. Was a clothier by trade, which he followed twelve years, when he purchased a farm in the town of Warren, Herkimer County, on which he continued to reside until 1863, when he became a resident of this village. Was married in 1821, but has no children.

ALVIN WEATHERBEE

WAS born in Hartland, Windsor County, Vermont, March 14th, 1794. Emigrated with his parents to the town of Warren, Herkimer County, in 1798, and settled at Page's Corners, where his father erected a tannery, and conducted the business many years. Alvin was employed in the tannery with his father, and at the age of twenty-four was married; has two sons and one daughter.

Mr. Brayton Weatherbee, proprietor of the well-known Weatherbee Mills, near this place, is the eldest son of Mr. Alvin Weatherbee.

WILLIAM B. IRELAND.

MR. IRELAND and family commenced visiting this place in 1845, as guests of the Spring House. In 1860 he purchased the cottage on the corner of Main and Church streets, where he continued to reside during the summer months until 1865, and died at his city residence, No. 35 Washington Square, New York, on the 18th of December of the latter year, aged sixty-five years. His widow, Mrs. A. S. Ireland, still owns and occupies the cottage in this village during the summer months.

MRS. HOUSE.

THERE is now living near the " Kyle," in the town of Warren, an aged lady by the name of House. Remembers distinctly the events connected with the last destruction of " Andrustown " in 1778, by the Indian chieftain Brant, and his coadjutors. Mrs. House was born at Fall Hill, near Little Falls, previous to the Revolution, and is now more than one hundred years of age. The writer recently had a very pleasant interview with this aged matron, and found her remarkably active and vivacious. She will probably see many more years.

It will be observed that Andrustown was three times destroyed by the Indians. Twice previous to the Revolution.

After destroying the place, the Indians fled in the direction of the " Little Lakes," to which point they were pursued by a party of colonists, but succeeded in making their escape. " Benton " says there were a few white families at the " Little Lakes," called Young's Settlement, and the principal man was " *Young*," the patentee (a Tory), to whom the lands had been granted by the crown in 1752.

HENRY TULLER, ESQ.,*

SON of William Tuller, was born in the town of Otsego, Otsego County, March 14th, 1799. Was a mechanic. Was married at the age of twenty-one to a daughter of Samuel Shipman, by whom he had four sons and four

---

* Alderman Ackley Tuller, of Rome, New York, is a son of Henry Tuller, Esq.

daughters, all now living. He became a resident of Rich-field Springs in 1836, and purchased the property now known as the "Tuller House," of which he was pro-prietor until recently. Was elected justice of the peace in 1844, and held the office four years. Was elected police justice in 1859, holding the office eight years. Mr. and Mrs. Tuller celebrated their "golden wedding" in 1870. Mrs. Tuller died in December, 1872.

ISAAC S. FORD

WAS born in Saulsbury, Herkimer County, December 1st, 1800. Was married in 1824, and became a resident of the town of Manheim, and was elected to the office of supervisor in 1832. Removed to the town of Richfield in 1836, where he became an active politician.

In 1862 he was appointed assistant assessor of Inter-nal Revenue by Salmon P. Chase, then Secretary of the Treasury, the duties of which office he discharged to the entire satisfaction of the people of this district.

Removed to this village in 1866, retiring from public life. Has two sons and four daughters

FLY CREEK VALLEY.

THE ranges of mountains lying between Otsego and Canadarago Lakes, are divided by a deep valley through which flows a stream called Fly Creek, which takes its rise in the highlands of the town of Otsego, near the southern line of the town of Springfield, about midway between the two lakes. Issuing from the earth near a rocky ledge, at first a purling rivulet, it starts on its way to the Susquehanna, gradually increasing in size and importance as it receives accessions from smaller streams, and peacefully winding its way through green pastures and by the grassy banks of exuberant meadows, through silent and secluded dells and forest shades, until it reaches a distance of about five miles, when it is appropriated to the uses of a dancing saw-mill. It is now a stream of considerable volume and rapid flow, and is used for mill purposes at intervals, until it finally enters the Oaks Creek, about seven miles south of Canadarago Lake. Along this entire valley can be seen a succession of beautifully cultivated farms with their neat houses and outbuildings, indicating the thrift and independence of the occupants. The hop is the principal product, and is extensively cultivated, the ample returns of which give a high and substantial value to real estate.

The village of Fly Creek is situated about three miles directly west from Cooperstown, and has a population of about two hundred. The New York Gazetteer of 1860 says, "At this place is a fork factory, with a capital of $75,000, employing thirty men; a pail factory; a manufactory of agricultural implements and machinery, employing a capital of 25,000; and a foundery and machine-shop, employing twenty-five men." * The same authority also says "the first child born in the town of Otsego was William Jarvis, at Fly Creek, in 1787." This region is certainly remarkable for the average longevity of its people. A correspondent of the "Republican," writing from Fly Creek, March 6th, 1873, says "from Fly Creek, taking in a circle with a radius of a mile, we have 14 from 80 to 94, and 26 from 70 to 80, in all 40, all of whom, with their present health, bid fair to see their one-

* I understand that the last-named enterprise only is now in operation (1873).

hundreth birthday." High up on the mountain-range, between Otsego Lake and the valley of Fly Creek, and nearly surrounded by the primitive forest, is what is known or supposed to have been a small lake at an early period, but now overgrown by a thick mass of tufted vegetation which entirely envelops its surface. This was originally called "The Fly," and from it the valley and village one and a half miles to the westward derive their names. Among the earliest settlers in this valley known to the writer, were David Marvin, Deacon North, John Clark, Alexander Lerow, Charles Bailey, Silas and Luther Williams,* John Patten, Titus Davidson, Platt St. John, Nehemiah Hinds, Jacob Johnson; † Erastus, Chester, and Thomas Taylor ; Ira Hyde, Asael Davidson, John Lumley, and George Roberts. In nearly every instance the lands originally taken up by the above names are still in the possession of their descendants. Near the old burying-ground at Fly Creek village, there is now standing an ancient-looking little cottage, that was erected in the year 1790 by a Mr. Jarvis, father of Hon. Kent Jarvis, of Masillon, Ohio, who was born here June 13th, 1801. In June, 1873, Mr. Jarvis celebrated his seventy-second birthday in this house, furnishing a sumptuous banquet to about one hundred guests, mostly residents of Fly Creek Valley.

"JONES' WOOD."

This beautiful grove of lofty maples occupies a commanding eminence on the south side of Main Street, to the east of the village, in the midst of which is embowered

---

* Descendants of Roger Williams, of Rhode Island.

† Jacob Johnson built the first saw-mill on Fly Creek, soon after the Revolution.

the neat and attractive " Swiss Cottage " of L. O. Jones, of New York. The location of this pretty cottage is most picturesque, overlooking the entire village of Richfield Springs and the valley of the Canadarago.

The charms of this delightful place are greatly enhanced during the summer season, by the presence of Mr. Jones and his family.

The sloping field between this cottage and the village presents a number of eligible sites for mansions or cottages, being bordered by a fine growth of young maples that pleasantly shade the street.

" MAPLEWOOD."

Two miles directly east from Richfield Springs, to the left of the highway, is the elegant stone mansion known as "Maplewood," the home of Mr. Frank White and family, late of Albany, N. Y. This large and rich estate lies at the base of " *Waiontha* " Mountain, and is bounded on the north by one of the " *Waiontha* " lakes. The mansion is surrounded by a vigorous growth of young maples, and other forest-trees; and is one of the most pleasantly located residences in this section of the country.

CHURCHES.*

THERE are five distinct church organizations in this place, with their respective houses of worship. Although we do not claim entire exemption from the moral obliquities peculiar to many places of popular summer resort,

* We have given sketches of the several churches, in the order of their organization.

we can safely assert that a high standard of moral and
religious sentiment pervades the people, for in no other
place of equal size or number of inhabitants, are church
organizations better sustained. And we do not claim
entire credit for the material prosperity of our places of
public worship, for we must here acknowledge that our
summer visitors are profuse in their contributions to this
object. As our church memberships are numerically far
below what they should be in proportion to the population, it will be seen at once, that in order to maintain a
high order of clerical talent, we must rely to a considerable extent on the material assistance rendered by our
city friends. And in behalf of the several religious soci-
eties, I can safely say that the numerous tokens of Christian liberality extended to our clergymen, are deeply
appreciated, not only by them, but also by the several
churches they represent.

The winter of 1874 will long be remembered by the
people of Richfield Springs and surrounding country for
the wonderful manifestation of the Divine Spirit, in the
conversion of over one hundred and fifty souls, and the
upbuilding of the Redeemer's kingdom here.

Large numbers have been added to the membership
of the churches, as the fruits of this revival.

PRESBYTERIAN CHURCH.

The Congregational Church of Richfield (now the
first Presbyterian) was organized at a meeting of citizens
of the town of Richfield, called for the purpose at the
house of Jacob Brewster, in said town, on the 2d day of
February, 1803, as the first Congregational Society of
Richfield. Jabez B. Hyde, Seth Allen, John Woodbury, Obadiah Beardsley, and Martin Luce, were the
first trustees of said society.

On the 12th day of September, 1803, a meeting was held at the house of Benjamin Corbin, in Richfield, at which time this church had its regular ecclesiastical organization. Rev. James Southworth, of Bridgewater, and Rev. John Spencer, of Vernon, assisted at its organization. Ebenezer Curtis was the first moderator and clerk, and Seth Luce first delegate to the Association.

The church society was not regularly incorporated until the 11th of June, 1813, at which time the meeting was held (as appears in the minutes) in the "Congregational meeting-house;" but when said house was built, the record does not show. This house was destroyed by fire in 1822.* The present house of worship, situated in the village of Richfield Springs, was built about the year 1825, while Rev. Charles Wadsworth was pastor of the church, who is also the first pastor mentioned in the records of the society. In May, 1844, the church withdrew from the Oneida Association, and united with the Otsego Presbytery on the accommodation plan, and continued in this relation till 1868, when, at a meeting called for the purpose, on the 6th day of June, the members of the church resolved by a unanimous vote to change its name from Congregational to Presbyterian. The first ruling elders elected were H. C. Walter, Wm. D. Griffin, John· Dana, and Robert Hall. The first deacons were John J. Edick and Pardon K. Hopkins. The following are the names of the pastors of the church, as nearly as can be ascertained from the imperfect records, and also the time of their pastorate: Rev. Charles Wadsworth, 1824 to 1830; Rev. D. Van Valkenburg, 1830 to 1844; Rev. W. C. Boyce, 1844 to 1846;

* This church stood in the western part of Monticello village near the cemetery.

Rev. T. B. Jervis, 1846 to 1852; Rev. Henry Boynton, as a temporary supply during the winter of 1852–3.

Rev. Charles Wadsworth, after an absence of about twenty-four years, returned in 1854, and remained till 1858. Mr. M. P. Hill, a student from Auburn Seminary, supplied the pulpit during the summer months of 1858 and 1859. Rev. Andrew Parsons, a student from Auburn Seminary, was ordained by Otsego Presbytery in June, 1860, and remained with the church as its pastor till the spring of 1866.

Rev. F. H. Seeley, a student from Auburn Seminary, was ordained by Otsego Presbytery in July, 1866, and immediately commenced his labors in this church, and is still its pastor. All the ministers mentioned in connection with this church, so far as known, are living at this date, except Rev. D. Van Valkenburg, who died while pastor of the church in Springfield, Nov. 24th, 1864, and now rests near the little church in this village, where for so many years his voice was heard proclaiming divine truth.

The Chapel connected with this church was built in 1870, at a cost of fifteen hundred dollars, which amount was bequeathed to the trustees of the society by the late Amasa Abbott, of Warren, Herkimer County, who died at the residence of his nephew, Allen Bloomfield, January 2d, 1868, aged sixty-eight years and seven months.

Present trustees of the society, John Dana, P. K. Hopkins, W. D. Griffin, H. C. Walter, H. M. De Long, W. T. Bailey.

THE FIRST UNIVERSALIST CHURCH.

(From the Records.)

At a meeting of a number of the inhabitants of Richfield and the adjoining towns, convened pursuant to previous public notice at the house of Cornelius M. Paul, in the town of Richfield, on the 23d day of May, 1833, for the purpose of organizing a Universalist Society; organized by choosing the Rev. Job Potter, moderator, and Tideman II. Gordon, clerk. The object of the meeting was then stated from the chair, when a ballot was had, and Davis Brown and Tideman II. Gordon were chosen to preside at this election, and to decide on the qualifications of voters. Resolved, That we elect five trustees. The meeting then proceeded to ballot for trustees, and on canvassing the votes, it appeared that Benjamin R. Elwood, James Wilson, George Tuckerman, Davis Brown, and Moses Wheeler received a unanimous vote, and were duly elected.

Tideman II. Gordon was elected Clerk.

Benjamin R. Elwood, Treasurer.

The trustees were then classed as follows:

First class—Davis Brown, Moses Wheeler.

Second class—James Wilson, George Tuckerman.

Third class—Benjamin R. Elwood.

The church edifice of the society is a substantial stone structure, and was erected in the year 1833, on grounds presented to the society by Nathan Dow, Esq.

FIRST MINISTERS.

According to the records, Rev. Orrin Roberts preached in this church two Sabbaths in each month, from April, 1834, to March, 1835, inclusive.

Rev. L. C. Brown preached one Sunday in each month, from April, 1835, to March, 1836, inclusive.

Rev. T. J. Smith engaged to preach one-half the time the ensuing year, commencing in the month of March, 1836.

From 1837 to 1861, the following clergymen preached in this church at intervals, viz.: J. S. Kibby, —— Belden, J. H. Tuttle, D. C. Tomlinson, W. E. Manley. In the spring of 1862, Rev. S. R. Ward was called as the regular pastor of the church, in which capacity he continued to labor until April, 1873, when he was called to the Second Universalist Church of Syracuse, where he is now stationed. During the pastoral labors of Mr. Ward, the church edifice was greatly enlarged and beautified, at an outlay of $11,000.

Rev. Mr. Cook, of Utica, is now the regular pastor.

EPISCOPAL CHURCH.

St. John's Church, Richfield Springs, Otsego County, N. Y., was organized according to law, on the 1st day of October, 1849. The Rev. Samuel G. Appleton, rector of Saint Luke's Church, Richfield, N. Y. (Monticello), on the morning of Sunday, the 23d day of September, 1849, at the residence of George B. Cary, celebrated Divine service, and gave public notice of the purpose to organize a parish in the village of Richfield Springs. A meeting was appointed to be held on the 1st day of October next ensuing, in the same place where the service was held, to carry out said purpose. On Sunday morning, the 30th day of September, the Rev. Mr. Appleton again celebrated Divine service at the residence of Mr. George B. Cary, and repeated the notice given on the previous Sunday.

On Monday, October 1st, 1849, at 3 o'clock in the afternoon, a number of persons assembled at the house above mentioned, and unanimously resolved to organize a parish in communion with the Protestant Episcopal Church in the United States of America, under the name and title of Grace Church. This resolution was afterwards reconsidered, and the name fixed as it at present continues, St. John's Church, Richfield Springs, N. Y.

The officers elected at this time were John W. Tunnicliff, Senior Warden, John Culbert, Junior Warden.

Vestrymen—William Hayes, George B. Cary, Elias Braman, Olcott C. Chamberlin, Erastus S. Belknap, Charles Delong, Price Griffith, Joshua Whitney.

At a meeting of the wardens and vestrymen, held on the 8th day of October, 1849, at the residence of George B. Cary, a committee of five persons was appointed for the purpose of circulating a subscription paper to secure funds for the erection of a church building. A. Tunnicliff, J. W. Tunnicliff, E. Braman, W. C. Crain, and G. B. Cary constituted this committee.

On Wednesday morning, August 21st, 1850, at 10 o'clock, the corner-stone of the present church building was laid with appropriate ceremonies, immediately after Divine service, by the Rev. Stephen II. Battin, rector of Christ Church, Cooperstown, N. Y. There were also present and assisting, the Rev. Joseph II. Price, D.D., and the Rev. Caleb S. Henry, D.D., of New York City, and the Rev. Robert Davis, of Philadelphia. The Rev. Samuel G. Appleton having removed to Delhi, Delaware County, N. Y., on the 7th of April, 1851, the vestry met, and appointed J. S. Davenport as a committee to go to New York and engage the Rev. Mr. Clements as rector of the parish. For some reason Mr. Clements did not accept the appointment. The Rev. Owen P. Thackara, from the Diocese of Maryland, became rector of the parish at some time during the spring or summer of 1851.

The incorporation of the church was approved by the Standing Committee of the Diocese during the year 1851, and the parish was received into union with the Convention of the Diocese. On the 11th day of August, 1853, the present church edifice was duly consecrated to the worship of the *Triune God* by the Rt. Rev. Jonathan Mayhew Wainwright, D.D., D.C.L. On the 3d day of August, 1854, Bishop Wainwright again visited the parish, preached, confirmed three, and addressed them ; and in the afternoon presided at a meeting of the Convocation of Delaware and Otsego counties.

Unfortunately there is no record preserved in the parish of the names of those confirmed at this time. Late in the year 1855, the Rev. Mr. Thackara ceased to hold services in the church, and the Rev. James W. Capen succeeded him. Mr. Capen's stay, however, was very brief. In June, 1856, the Rev. Robert T. Pearson took charge of the parish. On the 22d of April, 1857, the Rev. Mr. Thackara's resignation of the rectorship of the parish was accepted, and the Rev. Mr. Pearson was duly elected rector in his place. On the 7th day of August, 1856, the Rt. Rev. Horatio Potter, D.D., LL.D., made his first visitation of the parish, preached, and administered the Holy Communion.

To the Annual Convention of the Diocese, held in Sept. 1857, the Rev. Mr. Pearson made the first report ever made of the condition of the parish. There were then thirty-four families (about one hundred and fifty individuals) connected with the parish. The Sunday school had two teachers and fifteen scholars. On the 31st of July, 1858, the Rt. Rev. Bishop Potter visited the parish, preached, and confirmed thirteen persons.

In September of the same year, the Rev. Mr. Pearson records the number of communicants as twenty-eight. On the 22d of October, 1859, the Rev. Mr. Pearson resigned the rectorship of the parish. The church was closed from that date until the first Sunday in May of the following year.

On the 2d of May, 1860, the Rev. J. W. Capen was elected by the vestry as officiating minister until the vacancy in the rectorship should be filled. On the 31st of October, 1860, the Rev. Wm. J. Alger was elected rector of the parish. Although Mr. Alger accepted the call, there is no record of his having performed any duty in the parish at this time. On Friday, the 2d of August, 1861, the Rt. Rev. Bishop Potter visited the parish, preached, and confirmed two (one of them in private). To the Annual Convention in September the senior warden reported as follows, viz.: "During the year we have been without a rector. During the last winter we have had no services, except on two or three Sundays. Rev. J. W. Capen, returning home from Florida the last of May, has again supplied us with services as his health would permit. We have begun and will soon complete a very convenient and comfortable rectory." In 1862, the Rev. Charles L. Sykes took charge of the parish as missionary. On Sunday, the 26th day of July, 1863, the Rt. Rev. Bishop Potter visited the parish, preached, ordained the Rev. C. L. Sykes priest, and confirmed two persons. On Sunday, the 31st of July, 1864, the Rt. Rev. Bishop Potter visited the church, preached, and confirmed five persons.

On the 30th of July, 1869, the Rev. C. L. Sykes resigned the rectorship of the parish. In May, 1870, the Rev. Joshua R. Peirce became rector of the parish, and continued in the rectorship until October 1st, 1872. At this time the present incumbent, the Rev. Edward M. Pecke, entered upon his duties as rector of the parish. During the twenty-four years of the existence of the parish, so far as can be ascertained, 110 persons have been baptized, 41 have been confirmed, 60 have been married, and 45 have been buried. Connected with the parish at the present time, there are 46 families or parts of families, including about 175 individuals. The number of communicants is 42. The Sunday school numbers 35 children and 5 teachers.

The parish property consists of the church building (seating about 200 people, altogether inadequate to the wants of the worshippers in the summer season), and the lot upon which it stands; also a rectory opposite the church, with a large lot of ground about it; a bell, an organ, and all the appointments for a due performance of *Divine service.*

THE CATHOLIC (St. JOSEPH'S) CHURCH.

This church society was incorporated in 1853, with a membership of about 25.

It was at this time a mission station or branch of the church at Cooperstown.

The trustees—Patrick Weldon, James Nellis, and William Burke.

The first services of the society were held in the district school-house, and at the private residences of the members.

In the year 1870 the present church edifice was completed at a cost of 3,500, and dedicated to the worship of God, by the Rev. M. C. Devit, of Cooperstown. Present membership (1873) 200.

Trustees—Patrick Weldon, William Burke. Dimen-

sions of the church, 32 by 60 feet. Is situated on the
north side of Canadarago Street. Oldest member of the
church at this time, Mrs. Bridget King, aged 92 years.

THE FIRST METHODIST EPISCOPAL CHURCH.

"Previous to the year 1871, there was no organized
society of Methodists in this village. There were in the
vicinity several small chapels where services were occasionally held by Methodist ministers or circuit riders.
In what are known as the 'Old Warren Meeting-House'
and the 'Old Columbia Meeting-House,' the former one
mile, and the latter six miles distant from the village,
Methodist services had been occasionally held for very
many years; and in their secluded grave-yards scores of
wearied travellers are peacefully sleeping in the shadows
of the humble building in which it had been their delight to gather. At the hamlet of Little Lakes in Warren, three miles distant, was a pretty little church under
charge of a regular pastor, the Rev. Mr. Stanton. The
eagerness with which the people flocked to these little
churches whenever services were held in them, showed
that in this vicinity were all the elements necessary for
the formation of an active, vigorous society."

THE FIRST CHURCH.

The First Methodist Episcopal Church of Richfield
Springs was incorporated May 29th, 1871, and the fol-
lowing board of trustees was chosen, viz.: George B.
Cary, Josiah House, Lewis McCredy, Samuel B. St.
John, Hiram Getman, Hiram L. Fay, Timothy Green,
Ezra W. Badger, and Cornelius Ackerman. Rev. O. C.
Wightman, of Mohawk, who with his congregation had

just built a handsome new church at that place, was assigned to this charge, and at once entered upon his duties. The society entered heart and soul into the project for the building of the new church, worshipping meanwhile in Union Hall, their meetings being uniformly well attended.

The Corner-stone laid.—April 1st, 1872, a lot was purchased on the corner of Main and Manley streets, for which $2,000 was paid. The corner-stone of the new church was laid August 20th, 1872, in the presence of a large concourse of people, with appropriate ceremonies. The building committee consisted of the following gentlemen : Ezra W. Badger, chairman ; George B. Cary, and Hiram L. Fay.

The Building.—The building is of brick, 45 by 75 feet, with chancel in the rear 6 by 17 feet, and has one tower 120 feet in height, in which has just been placed a fine bell costing $550. There is also a fine large and well-lighted basement for the Sunday school and chapel purposes. The total cost of the church, including the lot, is about $17,000.

The Dedication.—This occurred on Tuesday, January 6th, 1874. The services were opened with prayer by the Rev. Mr. Shepard, of Ilion, after which a hymn was read by the Rev. O. C. Wightman. The doxology was sung by the Springfield choir. The Rev. B. I. Ives of Auburn, then preached an eloquent sermon from Matt. v. 16, " *Let your light so shine before men that they may see your good works, and glorify your Father which is in heaven.*"

The amount of indebtedness remaining on the church ($10,600) was promptly subscribed by those present. The Messrs. Remington, of Ilion, gave the munificent sum of $3,000 in various ways, and they have heretofore helped the church by loaning them money without interest, and otherwise laid the society under lasting obligations to them, which they gratefully acknowledge.

This church is indeed an ornament to our village, and of which we may justly as a community feel proud. Among the clergymen of the Methodist Episcopal Church present, were the Rev. Mr. Corse, presiding elder; Rev. B. I. Ives, of Auburn; Rev. A. G. Markham, pastor of the church; Rev. A. B. Gregg, of Jordon; Rev. O. C. Wightman, former pastor, now of Forestport, Oneida County, and Rev. Mr. Shepard, of Ilion.

Note.—In closing this brief sketch of the several churches, we wish to remark that there is one important phase connected with the general character of the great numbers who annually visit this place. We allude to the respectful reverence for the Sabbath. Throughout this entire day a profound quiet pervades the place, and the several houses of public worship are thronged by full and atten tive congregations. Such an exhibition of substantial and conserva- tive Christian sentiment, cannot be without its moral influence upon all classes, who may be thus led to a deeper regard for the vital claims of the Holy Sabbath upon all sentient, accountable intelligences.

INDIANS.

THE Indian will never cease to be an object of interest to the people of this country, as being the original inhabitant of its entire territory, and possessing many noble traits of character in his native state, which remained as a leading feature of their numerous tribes, until brought in contact with the moral perversions of European civilization. Driven from the shores of the Atlantic by the encroachments of the whites, their num- bers have been gradually reduced, until we now look upon the remnants of the tribes with increasing interest, as associated with the once powerful nations that roamed through the mountain forests and lake valleys of this region. There is at present but one family of aborigines residing within the limits of this village. They are from the *Abenaka* * Nation of St. Francis Indians of Canada. They may be seen almost daily in the boarding season, with their ingeniously wrought wares of baskets, bows and arrows, and other trinkets, which they, in their quiet, modest way, offer for sale.

SUNSET HILL.†

THE village of Richfield Springs is surrounded by many sightly and beautiful eminences, that overlook the entire village and lake scenery, and furnish most desirable locations for residences or villas.

Sunset Hill, an accessible and much frequented eminence, is situated immediately to the north, and commands an extensive and delightful view of the village at our feet, half hidden by the dark thick foliage of ornamental trees, above which the several towering church-spires point heavenward. Nature never painted a fairer picture than is here spread out before us.

The prospect extends through a long vista, over a range of many miles. Away to the south stretches the beautiful valley of the Canadarago, with the gleaming

* The name of this nation (*Abenaka*) signifies "Sun of the morning.

† The old moss-covered well on the summit of Sunset Hill, was dug by Aaron Abbott in 1799, who also built a "log-cabin" near it, on the northeast. Aaron Abbott was grandfather of the late Amasa Abbott, of this place, and also of Clinton Abbott, Esq., of Cedar Falls, Iowa.

lake lying deep between the ranges of rugged mountains on the east and west. Far over the sparkling waters we catch a glimpse of the forest outlines, lying against the distant horizon, scarcely distinguishable from the hazy clouds which envelop them. Dark-green fields, broken by copses of luxuriant foliage, outspreading farms, and neat farm-houses in the distance, form a picture of exquisite beauty to the lover of rural scenes. The evening sun, slowly and tremblingly descends beneath a canopy of transcendent hues of crimson and gold, tinging each soft feathery cloud with its most exquisite and charming shades; while to the north are rich rolling fields of pastoral beauty, set with cottages and neatly arranged buildings or mills, on the banks of a little stream that takes its rise beneath the shadows of gracefully sweeping willows that stand like silent sentinels on its gravelly banks.

On the eastern slope of this beautiful eminence are the grounds recently purchased by Hon. C. H. McCormick, of Chicago, as the site of a summer residence, soon to be erected. These grounds have already been thickly set with a great variety of fruit and ornamental trees.

PROSPECT HILL

Lies to the northwest. From this point, a most charming view is spread out before us. To the eastward the shadowy range of forest-clad mountains stretch away to the south, where the broad bosom of the lake, with the little emerald isle, lie peacefully in the distance: while directly before us is the village, with the placid waters of "Lake Clement" in the foreground.

Two new streets from Main, have recently been opened to this eminence, by the enterprising proprietor. (See *Frontispiece.*)

WAIONTHA MOUNTAIN

Is situated directly to the east of Richfield Springs, about two miles distant, and is boldly outlined against the eastern sky. After a slightly fatiguing ascent, we find ourselves elevated far above the surrounding country. "Get thee up into the top of Pisgah (Waiontha), and lift up thine eyes, westward and northward, and eastward and southward, and behold it with thine eyes." (Deut. iii. 27.) To the lover of nature this point offers a most picturesque and charming view in every direction. Far beneath us, the eye rests upon the most beautiful scenes of cultivated fertility and civilized refinement— wide-spreading farms, rich in all the elements of wealth and luxury, graceful undulations and lofty hills covered with wild forests, and seamed with rocky gorges worn in their sides by tumbling streams and leaping cascades. The hillsides are dotted with snowy flocks, and cattle are quietly grazing, or repose peacefully in the shades of isolated trees.

"The cattle upon a thousand hills are His."

The old pastures, rolling around the bases of the hills, look like the smoothly shaven lawns of some vast pleasure park. From this point we can look into nine different counties, viz. Otsego, Schoharie, Montgomery, Fulton, Hamilton, Herkimer, Oneida, Madison, and Chenango.

To the north the eye can take in a range of more than forty miles, embracing the Bear and Panther mountains, that lie beyond the Garoga and Fish lakes of Fulton County. To the northeast, a portion of the Adirondacks are visible, while the deep valley of the historic Mohawk stretches far away into the labyrinths of the mountain-ranges beyond.

Directly to the east, about ten miles, can be seen the bold prominence known as " Cape Wicoff," that over-looks Cherry Valley, with the "Sharon Hills" in the distance. To the southeast, we can look down into the beautiful valley of the Susquehanna, with its wood-covered mountains that bound it on the east. To the south is a succession of lofty hills and deep valleys, while to the west lies the valley of Canadarago Lake, with its ranges of hills and mountains beyond; and the entire village of Richfield Springs is in full view.

Six distinct lakes can be seen from the summit of Waiontha Mountain, viz. Otsego, Canadarago, Allen's, Young's, Weaver's, and Summit Lake. The last named is situated about five miles to the northeast, but almost entirely hidden from view by intervening hills and forests. This little lake, as its name implies, occupies a position on the dividing ridge between the valleys of the Mohawk and Susquehanna, discharging its waters both north and south into these valleys respectively. In the month of May, 1839, five young people were drowned in this lake. Six persons were crossing the lake in a small boat, and when near the shore, the boat suddenly sprang aleak, and, turning over, precipitated the whole party into the water. The names of those drowned were Abram Walter, Catharine and Nancy Walter, nieces of the above, and a Mr. Barringer and sister. A little daughter of Abram Walter clung to the boat and was rescued. Abram Walter was a brother of Mr. Jacob Walter, of this village.

A short distance to the west of Summit Lake is a deep *sink*, called the "Kyle," into which a considerable stream of water flows, and disappears in a subterranean passage for several miles, and again appears on the surface near Van-Hornsville.* This sink is tunnel-shaped, about two hundred feet in circumference and fifteen feet deep. After heavy rains, it is sometimes filled with water, which, while it sinks away, moves round in rapid gyrations. On the estate of the late Col. Crain, about three miles to the west of the "Kyle," are several cavities of similar character, one of which is said to be fifty feet deep. At the base of Waiontha Mountain, to the northeast, lie the twin lakes called by the Indians *Wa-i-on-tha,†* a few rods apart, but united by a liquid ribbon, and holding in their embrace a quiet little hamlet, with its white church-spire, and adjacent church-yard with its monumental stones. One of these lakes is nearly hid from view from this point, by an intervening eminence of woodland on the estate of Mr. John E. Dalphin.

A few rods to the south lies Allen's Lake, a little circular basin, sparkling in the sunlight, and fringed with evergreens. The water of this lake is very pure, being fed exclusively by mountain springs. We trust that at no distant day this beautiful lake will be appropriated as a reservoir for the supply of water to Richfield Springs, as it lies three hundred feet above the village. Near the outlet of this lake stands an antiquated little saw-mill, showing that the flow of water must be considerable to answer its requirements. A variety of large and excel-

---

* Near this place, the early settlers found a large hemlock-tree entirely petrified. Also a gas spring, the vapor of which could be easily ignited.

† From which the mountain takes its name. At Van-Hornsville is a rocky "cave," much frequented by the guests of the Springs.

lent fish are found in its waters. On the summit of Waiontha Mountain, is a beautifully level plateau of several acres, covered with a fine, vigorous growth of young forest-trees; and it seems to be admirably adapted by nature for pleasure-grounds. Its extreme altitude of over seven hundred feet above the village, accessibility, and proximity to Richfield Springs, will no doubt soon call the attention of our citizens to the necessity of preparing it as a place of resort for the guests of the village. We may regard it as a good specific for indigestion, to ascend these high latitudes, and breathe the pure air of heaven, so full of electric life and vigor. It is indeed delightful to stand upon these elevated places of the earth, deeply impressed with the pleasurable emotions of freedom, in this our temporary *isolation*. We naturally grow into a liking of the country, with its fresh and bracing air, and the sparkling dew that at sunrise covers the hills and valleys with a profusion of brilliant diamonds; the wild rivers that silently wind among the hills, or bathe the feet of the mountains; the shaggy mists that lie in the twilight like unravelled clouds, lost upon the distant meadows; and we love especially the romantic hills, climbing in verdant beauty toward the sky, or, stretching in the dim distance, their soft blue smoky outlines. We love the lofty forest-trees that lift their broad arms toward heaven, and sway gently in the summer's breeze; we love the breadth and magnitude of the unrestrained liberty of country life, that kindles within our hearts the most exalted emotions of gratitude, and reverence for the true and the natural.

> " Thou who wouldst see the lovely and the wild
> Mingled in harmony on nature's face,
> Ascend our rugged mountains. Let thy foot
> Fail not with weariness, for on their tops

The beauty and the majesty of earth,
Spread wide beneath, shall make thee to forget
The steep and toilsome way. There as thou stand'st,
The haunts of men below thee, and around
The mountain summits, thy expanding heart
Shall feel a kindred with that loftier world
To which thou art translated, and partake
The enlargement of thy vision.
Thou shalt look upon the green and rolling forest-tops,
And down into the secrets of the glens, and streams,
That with their bordering thickets strive
To hide their windings. Thou shalt gaze, at once,
Here on white villages, and tilth, and herds,
And swarming roads, and there on solitudes
That only hear the torrent, and the wind,
And eagle's shriek."

WAIONTHA OBSERVATORY.

Under the authority of the citizens of Richfield Springs, an observatory is now being erected on the summit of Waiontha Mountain. It is designed especially for the pleasure of our summer visitors, and is free to all. This structure is an open frame-work of wood seventy feet in height, standing far above the surrounding forest-trees. This point is said to be the highest in the State, except the "Adirondacks," and from the top of this observatory on a clear day will be visible a vast and beautiful expanse of hill, dale, lake, and plain, spread like a map in every direction before the beholder.

RUM HILL.

There are several prominent points in this vicinity from which extensive and beautiful views can be obtained. Of these, "Rum Hill" is doubtless one of the most popular places of resort for the guests of the Springs, being very accessible from the highway leading from Allen's Lake to Cooperstown. It is situated about two miles directly south from Waiontha Mountain.

MOHEGAN HILL.

ABOUT one mile to the southwest of Waiontha stands Mohegan Hill, partly divested of the dense forests that once enveloped its entire summit. From this point a charming view is presented of the deep valley, lake, and village. This summit is six hundred and fifty feet above the village of Richfield Springs. Standing against the horizon, to the west, are the bold outlines of the blue hills of the town of Exeter, that appear like the rolling waves of the restless ocean.

At the western base of Mohegan Hill stands the farm residence of Mr. John Derthick.

GANO'S HILL,

RECENTLY laid out into village lots and sold to individuals, lies to the westward and south of Main Street. From this point a fine view is obtained in every direction. Several neat residences have already been erected in this locality.

CANADARAGO HILL.

THIS abrupt prominence, or steppe, seems to have been lifted up by some mysterious agency, from the level plain by which it is surrounded. A carriage driveway, of one half mile, has been cut around its sloping sides, and its summit graded to a level plateau, and neatly set with many young trees ; a most desirable site for a mansion or pavilion.   The railroad depot buildings are located at the western base of this eminence.

WILDER'S HILL.

This eminence is situated directly to the east, and is one mile distant from the centre of the village.   The residence of Mr. George Wilder occupies the summit, and is one of the most pleasantly located residences in this vicinity, overlooking the entire village and valley to the westward.   Wilder's Hill, with its long gradual slope toward the village, furnishes many desirable sites for residences, being bounded on the north by a beautiful native forest of a great variety of trees and shrubbery.

PANTHER'S MOUNTAIN.

This is an elevated point, situated about one mile to the southeast, still clothed in all its primitive beauty of dense forest-trees and shrubbery, reaching far down into the valley below.   It was the favorite hunting-ground of the Indian "Panther," who delighted in its wildness and seclusion.

This mountain, together with the contiguous range to the southward, still abounds in a variety of game. As we enter its deep shades, dark with the foliage of midsummer, and vocal with the notes of feathered songsters and the monotonous hum of insect life, the gentle breeze sighs through the topmost branches of the lofty forest trees, and the wild-pigeon coos in the beechen boughs over our heads; the saucy little squirrel chatters in his hemlock ambush close by, and the partridge whirs rapidly away from the tangled copse invaded by our feet, or greets us with his drum from his mossy retreat. To the west lies the placid Canadarago Lake, and to the north is the village of Richfield Springs, partly hidden by the thick foliage of ornamental trees and shrubbery that adorn the grounds of the residences and shade the streets and walks in every direction.

Against the western horizon are outlined the retreating mountain-tops, forming a background of great beauty. Scattered in every direction are rich farms, with their broad fields golden with grain or russet with stubble, white with fragrant buckwheat or emerald with carpets of clover, while the white and elegant farm-houses, surrounded by shading copses of clean and clustering maples, or relieved against the dense foliage of fruit-laden orchards, complete the exquisite picture of mingled rusticity and high civilization.

We love to ramble in the lone retreats of the forest, as "there is a pleasure in the pathless wood," for here we can muse with fair Nature, and be blest by her mild and gentle sympathy.

BENNET'S HILL

STANDS one and a half miles to the west of the Springs, and is crowned by the old-fashioned but substantial farm-house of Mr. Elijah Bennet.

This house is opened to guests through the summer season, and we can assure our city friends that they will find under this hospitable roof all the genuine products of the farm, and every convenience for families, besides ample room for exercise in the open fields, or for rambling in the romantic retreats of the forest.

There are many fine views from several points on this farm.

STOWEL HOUSE.

This large and elegant farm-house is situated near the " Walnut Grove," on the east bank of the lake, which it overlooks. The house is open to guests through the boarding season, and is a very desirable and pleasant home for those who seek the quiet retirement of the country. Harvey Stowel, Esq., proprietor.

GANO'S GROVE.

Near the western boundary of the corporation of this village is a beautiful grove, composed of a great variety of large indigenous forest-trees, covering an area of about six acres of elevated level ground, and bounded on the west by a deep ravine, through which runs the Delaware, Lackawanna and Western Railroad, in its approach to the village. In the year 1869, a stock company was organized by the following gentlemen, for the purpose of opening this grove to public use, and preparing it for pleasure parties, picnics, etc.: Hon. Louis Lawrence, James H. Gano, Hon. A. R. Elwood, Morgan Bryan, Dr. N. Getman, N. K. Ransom, E. W. Badger, Esq.

The small trees and shrubbery were removed, walks were opened, and steps made leading from the railroad to the grounds above. Several rustic buildings and a large platform for dancing were also constructed. The situation of this grove is charmingly delightful, and easy of access from the village. Directly opposite the grove on the north is the residence of James H. Gano, Esq., the proprietor of these beautiful grounds. This sylvan retreat presents a brilliant picture on a bright summer day, when filled with many joyous faces and merry tripping feet of happy children, who resort hither from the thronged cities to enjoy the gentle zephyrs that bring grateful coolness to the heated brow, and give bounding health and vigor to the frame of those of maturer years and more sedate proclivities. In the month of July, 1870, Prof. Squires made a balloon ascension from this grove.

POPULAR DRIVES FROM RICHFIELD SPRINGS.

CHERRY VALLEY.

Ascending the eminence to the east of Richfield Springs, over which Main Street leads, the tourist will find a most delightful drive along the high and substantial turnpike that leads through a rich farming district. Passing between the two little lakes, thence to the north of Otsego Lake, which can be seen a short distance to the south of Springfield, we soon reach the historic grounds of Cherry Valley, distant from the Springs about twelve miles.

At the commencement of the Revolution, Cherry Valley was still a frontier settlement. Lossing says, "Cherry Valley derived its name, according to Campbell, from the following circumstance." Mr. Dunlop, the venerable pastor (whose family suffered at the time of the massacre in 1788), engaged in writing some letters, inquired of Mr. Lindesay (the original proprietor of the soil) where he should date them, who proposed the name of a town in Scotland. Mr. Dunlop, pointing to the fine wild-cherry trees, and to the valley, replied, " Let us give our place an appropriate name, and call it Cherry Valley ;" which was readily agreed to. (*Annals of Tryon County.*) Late in the autumn of the above year, Cherry Valley was attacked by the Tories and Indians under the lead of Butler and Brant, and a horrible massacre ensued. * The family of Robert Wells, father of the late John Wells of New York, consisting of twelve persons, were brutally murdered; and one of the Tories boasted that he killed Mr. Wells † while at prayer. John Wells, the only member of the family who escaped, was at school in Schenectady at the time. The wife and daughter of Mr. Dunlop, Mrs. Dickson, and the wife and four children of Mr. Mitchel, were murdered in cold blood. Thirty-two of the inhabitants, mostly women and children, and sixteen Continental officers and soldiers, were killed ; the residue of the inhabitants were taken prisoners and carried off, and all the buildings in the place were burned. All the frontier settlements were ravaged, and nearly every building, except those belonging to Tories, was burned. At the time the place was destroyed, James S. Campbell, father of Hon. W. W. Campbell, author of " The Annals of Tryon County," was a child six years of age, and was taken captive to-

---

* The policy of the British Government, in appealing to the cupidity of the Indian tribes, by extravagant offers of reward for the scalps of the colonists, was deprecated by the Christian world. But we are glad to know that a few noble spirits in Parliament, among which were Pitt and Chatham, opposed this cruel measure with all the power that moral philosophy and eloquence could command.

† The present residence of Mr. Joseph Phelon occupies the site of the original dwelling of Mr. Wells.

gether with his mother and several other members of the family. Lossing says, " The children of Mrs. Campbell were all restored to her at Niagara except this one. In June, 1780, she was sent to Montreal, and there she was joined by her missing boy. He had been with a tribe of the Mohawks, and had forgotten his own language ; but he remembered his mother, and expressed his joy at seeing her, in the Indian language. She lived until 1836, being then ninety-three years of age. She was the last survivor of the Revolutionary women in the region of the headwaters of the Susquehanna." Her son, Hon. James S. Campbell, died at Cherry Valley,* March 23d, 1870, aged ninety-eight years.

About two miles to the north of Cherry Valley, in a field to the left of the road leading to the Mohawk, is what is known as "Brant's Rock," near which Lieut. Wormwood was shot and scalped by the notorious Indian chief Brant during the Revolution.

At the time of the destruction of Cherry Valley, in a westerly direction about one mile resided Mr. Clyde and family, who almost miraculously escaped the fate of the victims already noticed. The father early sought, on hearing of the common danger, to join the brave defenders of the settlement; but on nearing the house of Mr. Wells, was driven back by the savages, a portion of whom had already taken the field leading to his home. His family fled, escaping to a high point of land covered by a dense forest. A daughter became separated from the others, and after being exposed several hours to the cold

---

* By the liberality of a Christian lady of Cherry Valley, a stone church and lecture-room of extraordinary beauty, style, and workmanship, costing $30,000, was recently presented to the Presbyterian church and society of the above place, which will stand as a monument to her memory many years after she has passed from the shores of time.

of a November night, was finally sought out and brought
back by a soldier, from whom she attempted to flee, supposing him to be an enemy. She bore away in her arms
an infant brother of six years, the grandfather of the now
living Mr. Jefferson Clyde, of Cherry Valley, to whom
we are indebted for valuable facts in relation to the early
settlement of this section.

In a recent visit to Cherry Valley, we were not a little
surprised to find that no *monument* marked the burial-
place of these early martyrs, except one modest slab of
marble that tells the sad story of the fearful day: "In
memory of the brave Colonel 'Ichabod Alden,' native
of Danbury, Massachusetts, who was murdered by the
savages in this place, on the 11th day of November,
1778, in the thirty-second year of his age." With wondering regret we looked for something pointing to the
place where the massacred fathers, mothers, grown-up
sons and daughters, the hoary-headed grand-parents, and
infant children were buried. Tradition points to a depression in the ground where the thirty-two were interred
in one common grave; and as it is feared by the writer
that the neglect of the past may continue to the utter
oblivion of this sacred spot, he would record that eight
feet to the west of the grave of the thirty-two murdered
inhabitants, there stands a square marble shaft, about seven
feet high, inscribed, "To Sarah Wilson, who died in
1778, aged thirty-six years."

Immediately after the close of the Revolution, the
individuals and families that escaped from Cherry Valley
during the war, returned again to their homes, and the
place was soon rebuilt and occupied by other settlers
also, and was for many years the principal settlement in
Otsego County, furnishing to the country some of its
most distinguished men, among whom were—John Wells

Esq., the distinguished lawyer of New York city; Hon. W. W. Campbell, author of "Annals of Tryon County;" Rev. Eliphalet Nott; Jabez D. Hammond, Esq., author of "Political History of New York;" Hon. Levi Beardsley, author of "Reminiscences of Otsego;" Hon. Judge Seeley; Alvan Stewart, Esq.; James O. Morse, Esq. Also, Dr. Joseph White, and his two sons, Delos and Menzo White, who were three of the most distinguished surgeons of the country. On the occasion of the funeral of Dr. Menzo White, the clergyman, Rev. Mr. Nichols, pointing in the direction of the late "office" * of the deceased, remarked, "Yonder office, the modern '*Bethesda*,' the ramifications of whose healings were well-nigh as multitudinous as the 'catacombs' of ancient *Rome*."

The beautiful village of Cherry Valley is situated near the headwaters of Cherry Valley Creek, in the extreme northeastern part of Otsego County, and has a population of about 1,500. This is the present terminus of the railroad from Cobleskill, on the Albany and Susquehanna road via Sharon Springs to Cherry Valley.

Efforts are now being made to continue this railroad west to Richfield Springs (*surveys having already been made*), connecting with the Delaware, Lackawanna and Western, thus opening to the latter point a shorter and more direct communication with the city of Albany, distant only sixty-five miles.

SOLDIERS' MEMORIAL.

A MARBLE monument, about twenty feet high, of beautiful execution and proportions, and crowned by an eagle, stands in a public centre in this village. Upon

---

* The office of Dr. Menzo White is now occupied by his nephew, Dr. Joseph White, a popular and skilful practitioner.

the four sides of this monument are inscribed the principal battles in which thirty-five of the brave souls of Cherry Valley "*died that their country might live;*" viz. Antietam, Fredericksburg, Gettysburg, second Bull Run, Cold Harbor, Winchester, Wilderness, Petersburg.

6th N. Y. Cavalry.—Sergt. Philo D. Chaddenden, Jacob Hardendorf, John Beaumont, Sergt. James H. Moore, Samuel Bates.

121st N. Y. Infantry.—Sergt. John Daniels, James Sherman, Jabez D. Wilson, Sergt. Edward Wales, Geo. N. L. Drake, Joseph B. Howe, John W. Ballard.

U. S. Navy.—George P. Engell, Col. and Brev. Gen. Cleveland J. Campbell.

1st Regt. U. S. S. S.—Capt. Charles D. McLean, Dwight Reed, Henry T. Ferguson, Sergt. Wm. O. McLean, Charles Gould.

U. S. N.—Charles P. N. Nuhall.

104th N. Y. I.—John Barker.

2d N. Y. H. A.—John H. Bush.

1st N. Y. C.—John F. Bottsford.

6th N. Y. H. A.—Salmon Drake.

152d N. Y. I.—Geo. Nelson, Cornelius Hardendorf, Geo. Van De Bogart.

44th N. Y. I.—Corp. James H. Drake, John Wallace.

76th N. Y. I.—Capt. Robert Story, 1st Lieut. Barnard Phenis, Wm. Sterns Bradford, J. D. Fox.

8th N. Y. C.—W. C. Crafts, 1st Lieut.

MRS. STOWE

SAYS (in 1872), "Cherry Valley to-day is an innocent, quiet Arcadia, lying within an hour's distance of three of the most fashionable summer watering-places, so that a short ride may bring you in sight of all the pomps and vanities that one may desire to see. Sharon Springs and Richfield now rival Saratoga in attraction, and number their thousands. Cooperstown is another most attractive and much-frequented point.

"We visited Richfield, and passed a day very pleasantly. It is a village of hotels and boarding-houses, and it was said three thousand visitors were there summering. There is a spring there whose waters we should think would be sufficient to frighten anybody away that ever tasted them, evidently either sulphurated or phosphorated hydrogen. One would think that it must have been bored down into some antediluvian stratum of spoiled eggs. Yet drinking of this spring appears to be one of the things to do in Richfield. We understand that ladies enamelled with bismuth, arsenic, and other minerals have occasionally been turned all sorts of colors by the vapor of this spring.

"What if there were a moral test of all shams equally searching! For the rest, Richfield has a high, pure air, which is said to be very health-giving; and it is a fact, we are told, that people who once begin to go there come back year after year with increasing interest."

GENERAL CLINTON'S EXPEDITION.

"In the spring of 1779, it was determined to send a formidable force into the Indian country of Western New York, for the purpose of chastising the savages and their Tory allies so thoroughly that the settlements upon the Mohawk and the upper branches of the Susquehanna might enjoy a season of repose. The tribes of the Six Nations were then populous. They had many villages, vast corn-fields, and fruitful orchards and gardens in the fertile country westward of Otsego Lake. It was supposed that the most effectual method to subdue or weaken them would be to destroy their homes and lay waste their fields, and thus drive them farther back into the wilderness toward Lake Erie. Already the Mohawks had been thrust out of the valley of their name, and their families were upon the domains of the Cayugas and Senecas. It was, therefore, determined to make a combined movement upon them of two strong divisions of military, one from Pennsylvania and the other from the north, at a season when their fields and orchards were fully laden with grain and fruits. It was a part of the plan of the expedition to penetrate the country to Niagara, and break up the nest of vipers there. General Sullivan was placed in the chief command, and led in person the division that ascended the Susquehanna from Wyoming, while General Clinton commanded the forces that penetrated the country from the mouth of the Canajoharie. It was arranged to unite the two divisions at Tioga. Clinton's troops, fifteen hundred strong, were mustered at Canajoharie on the 15th of June, and on the 17th he commenced the transportation of his bateaux and provisions across the hilly country to Springfield, at the head of Otsego Lake, a distance of more than twenty miles. It was an arduous duty, for his boats numbered two hundred and twenty, and he had provisions sufficient for three months. He reached Springfield, with all his baggage, on the 30th. On his way he captured Hare and Newberry, two notorious spies, the former a lieutenant in the British service, and the latter the miscreant who murdered Mr. Mitchel's wounded child at Cherry Valley.

"They were tried, and hanged, pursuant to the sen-

8

tence of the court, and to the entire satisfaction of the inhabitants of the country. Clinton with his division proceeded to the foot of Otsego Lake, and there awaited orders from Sullivan. A day or two after his arrival, General Schuyler communicated to him the important information that the purpose of the expedition was known to the enemy, and that four hundred and fifty regular troops, one hundred Tories, and thirty Indians had been sent from Montreal to reinforce the tribes against whom it was destined. This information General Schuyler received from a spy whom he had sent into Canada. The spy had also informed him that they were to be joined by one-half of Sir John Johnson's regiment and a portion of the garrison at Niagara. On the 5th, Mr. Dean, the Indian interpreter, arrived with thirty-five Oneida warriors, who came to explain the absence of their tribe, whom Clinton, by direction of Sullivan, had solicited to join him. They confirmed the intelligence sent by Schuyler, and added that a party of Cayugas and Tories, three hundred in number, were then upon the war-path, and intended to hang upon the outskirts of Clinton's army on its march to Tioga. Clinton remained at the south end of Otsego Lake, awaiting the tardy movements of Sullivan, until the first week in August. His troops became impatient, yet he was not idle. He performed a feat which exhibited much ingenuity and forecast. He discovered that in consequence of a long drought, the outlet of the lake was too inconsiderable to allow his boats to pass down upon its waters. He therefore raised a dam across it at the foot of the lake, by which the waters would be so accumulated, that when it should be removed, the bed of the outlet would be filled to the brim, and bear his boats upon the flood.

" The work was soon accomplished, and in addition to

the advantages which it promised to the expedition, the damming of the lake caused great destruction of grain upon its borders, for its banks were overflowed, and vast corn-fields belonging to the Indians were deluged and destroyed. The event also greatly alarmed the savages. It was a very dry season, and they regarded the sudden rising of the lake, without any apparent cause, as an evidence that the Great Spirit was displeased with them. And when Clinton moved down the stream with his large flotilla upon its swollen flood, the Indians along its banks were amazed, and retreated into the depths of the forest." (*Lossing's Revolution.*)

COOPERSTOWN.

THE site of this village was first seen by an Anglo-Saxon in the year 1737. The next visit made to this point, of which we have any record, was the expedition of General Clinton, previously noticed. The village of Cooperstown was first settled by Judge Wm. Cooper,* about the year 1790, and was incorporated in 1807 as the village of Otsego; but its name was changed to Cooperstown in 1812. It has been the county seat from its first settlement to the present time.

In the summer of 1784, General Washington, in company with General George Clinton and several other officers of the U. S. army, leaving the Mohawk River at Canajoharie, visited Cherry Valley and Otsego Lake, then surrounded by the deep solitudes of an unbroken wilderness. Cooperstown, at the present time, is one of the most beautiful villages of Central New York. It lies in a deep valley, at the south end of Otsego Lake, bor-

* Father of James Fenimore Cooper.

dered on the east and west by wood-covered mountains that stretch far away to the north and south. The village has a population of about two thousand. Since the completion of the railroad to this point from the Albany and Binghamton road, sixteen miles distant, it has become a place of popular resort through the summer months, for pleasure-seekers and invalids who desire the high mountain air of the country.

Cooperstown is amply supplied with large and commodious hotels,* and every facility for the entertainment of guests. It has the purest of water, delightful walks and drives, and the most romantic and picturesque natural scenery in this portion of the State. On the western shore of Otsego Lake are several delightful points, that present some of the most beautiful views to be found in this region. The Three-mile-point House † is very pleasantly located, overlooking the lake and village of Cooperstown. Directly in front is the wood covered projection known as " Three-mile" or " Wild-rose Point." " A favorite resort for picnics. Upon this spot have congregated in merry dance the old and young, from almost every quarter of the globe." " *Ay !* water you shall have, if you drink the lake dry. I'll just carry you down to it, that you may drink your fill." " Here he first helped him to take an attitude in which he could appease his burning thirst." (*Deerslayer*).

Hon. Samuel Nelson, Judge of the Supreme Court of the United States, was a resident of Cooperstown. Died December 12th, 1873, aged eighty years.

Cooperstown and Richfield Springs are now inti-

---

* Of the number of hotels of the place, we may mention the " Cooper House," the " Central," the " Fenimore," and Carr's Hotel, as being among the largest and most commodious of the country.

† A. W. Thayer, proprietor.

Five-mile Point, *Otsego Lake*.

mately connected by a line of steamboats,* on Otsego
Lake, 9 miles, and omnibuses to Richfield, 7 miles. We
trust the time is not far distant when the railroad will
be continued from Cooperstown to Richfield Springs,
thus forming a connection with the railroad to this place.

"THE FIVE-MILE-POINT HOUSE."

In the year 1847 a carriage road was opened along the
western shore of Otsego Lake, cut in the steep sides of
the banks near the water's edge. This wild and beautifully shaded road now forms one of the most delightful
drives to be found in this whole region.

In 1850 a public house † was erected at what is now
popularly known as the "Five-mile Point," by Mr. J. D.
Tunnicliff, its present gentlemanly proprietor. This is
one of the most romantic and picturesque places of resort
to be found on the gravelly shores of the lake. The
level lawn and open grounds of this house extend far out
into the lake, and are pleasantly shaded by gigantic oaks
and other forest-trees, whose dark outlines are distinctly
reflected in the deep bosom of the transparent waters.

A fleet of row-boats are to be seen moored on the
gravelly beach, with every convenience for the sports of
the angler.

The lake abounds in a great variety of most excellent
fish, among which the famous "Otsego bass" far tran-
scend in quality all others known to the civilized world,
and are found only in the waters of this lake. Having

* The "Natty Bumppo" and "Pioneer."
† This public house is a favorite stopping-place for the guests of
Richfield Springs, on their way to Cooperstown.

secured your fish, you can have them cooked in marvellous style in the *cuisine* of the excellent hotel, together with a great variety of epicurean luxuries, known as "*game dinners.*" A short distance to the west of Five-mile Point, in the rugged mountain-forest, is what is known as the " Cañon," still to be seen in all its pristine beauty, through which rushes a rapidly flowing stream, tumbling over rocky beds of limestone ledges, as it hurries on toward the tranquil bosom of the " Haunted Lake." " 'Twas through this cañon, ' Deerslayer ' * made his escape when pursued by the Hurons." " The Hurons were whooping and leaping behind him. He saw by the formation of the land that a deep glen intervened before the base of a second hill could be reached. A fallen tree lay near him, in a line parallel to the glen, at the brow of the hill: to leap on it took but a moment. Previous to disappearing from his pursuers, however, Deerslayer stood on the height, and gave a cry of triumph, as if exulting at the sight of the descent that lay before him." (*Deerslayer*, xxvii.)

" The Five-mile Point is the place selected by ' Hetty ' for landing, after her escape from the Ark. The point in question was the first projection that offered on that side of the lake where a canoe, if set adrift with a southerly air, would float clear of the land, and where it might be no great violation of probabilities to suppose it might even hit the Castle. Such then was Hetty's intention, and she landed on the extremity of the gravelly point, beneath an overhanging oak." (*Deerslayer.*)

---

* *Cooper's works.* Views of Otsego Lake scenery, by W. G. Smith, of Cooperstown, for sale at the *Five-mile-point House.*

OTSEGO LAKE AND COOPER.

Six miles directly east from Richfield Springs, over a delightfully pleasant highway, brings us to the beautiful and historic "Otsego Lake," stretching itself entirely across the valley between the lofty ranges of wood-covered mountains that bound it on the east and west, and extending from the "Sleeping Lion" on the north to the Otsego Rock, near the outlet on the south, a distance of about nine miles.

OTSEGO LAKE.

BY MRS. S. J. DOUGLASS.

All hail, fair Otsego! thou beautiful lake,
With thy green wooded slopes, fringed with fern and with brake,
And " Wellington Mountain," towering so high,
Stands poised like an eagle, close to the sky;
Yes, he stands like a monarch in royal array,
When the sunlight comes up to the rim of the day,
Casting bright splendor all over thy face,
Till it ripples and dimples with wonderful grace;
Then the gold of the sun and the woods' emerald green
Harmoniously blend with thine own silver sheen;
And at night, when the moonlight peeps out from the cloud,
Each star is reflected, each leaf is endowed
With thy magical beauty, thy fairy-like charm,
While each wave lies asleep on thy bosom so calm.
Then the Cooperstown spires reflect in thy blue,
And the fleecy white clouds drop down diamonds of dew,
Which embroider thy banks like the robe of a queen,
Setting here a pearl dewdrop and there a moonbeam,
With such delicate skill, that a Rembrandt might pine
To be able to picture such beauty as thine.
Not " Afton's sweet water," nor " Elgin," nor " Ayr,"
Nor Burns' " Bonny Doon," can with thee compare;
And Byron may sing, in his praise of the " Rhine,"
There are classical beauties which only are thine;

And Cooper has made thee immortal we know,
For we read of thy charms in the long, long ago ;
And we'll echo the song of thy praises again
Till woodland and mountain and valley and glen
Shall join in the anthem, shall swell the refrain,
While the winds bear it back to thy bosom again,
To dash up the waters in white-caps and roar
Like the sound of the sea on the wave-beaten shore.

Writing from Cooperstown, a correspondent says :
"I confess to a weakness for visiting the houses and
haunts of men of genius. Nothing in the world drew
me here but the fact that it was the place where Cooper,
the great novelist, lived, died, and was buried. I wished
to see the scenes so graphically described in the ' Pioneer,'
and other Leatherstocking tales, and to visit the spot
where the great master drew so much of inspiration.

"I had heard much about the loveliness of the place,
and for once fame has not overshot the mark. The situation is most picturesque. Cooperstown is embowered in
the sweetest of little valleys, amid mountain views, at the
source of the Susquehanna River. It has a rich valley
on the one side, and the Otsego Lake on the other. This
lake is not unworthy of the appellation bestowed upon
it by Cooper, of ' Glimmerglass,' for the wonderful
transparency of its waters. On its eastern shores extend
a range of mountains from five to six hundred feet high,
densely wooded. On the western shore the hills are less
high, less rugged, but hardly less picturesque."

CLASSIC SCENES—THE LEATHER-STOCKING TALES.

The shores of this lake are classic. Every cove and
rocky glen is hallowed by tender memories. Here are
located some of the most thrilling scenes in the "Leatherstocking" tales. Here glorious "Natty Bumppo," first

as the youthful "Deerslayer," afterwards as the aged "Leatherstocking," loved the dark-eyed Judith Halter, and rescued from the panther's claws the fair form of "Elizabeth Temple." Here the curious traveller may explore the depths of "Leatherstocking's Cave," visit the scenes of the fight with the panther, and the site of Muskrat Castle. So true was Cooper to life, so faithful to nature are his pictures, that every curve and indentation of the shore and every sweep of the hills is familiar to the reader of the "Pioneer" and "Deerslayer." It requires no great stretch of fancy to people the scenes with wraiths of old "Haller," "Harry Hussy," the gentle "Hetty," "Wah-ta-wah" the Indian maiden, "Natty," and the rest of the deathless concourse. Otsego is fitly called the "Haunted Lake."

MEMENTOS OF COOPER—HIS FAMILY.

Family aristocracies are short-lived in *America*. Judge Cooper, father of the novelist, was a petty landed baron in his time. He was virtually the founder of the place, over whose few inhabitants he exercised a mild species of lorddom. He was a man of courtly manners, lived in what in those days was considered a stately mansion, and entertained distinguished company, numbering among his guests a no less illustrious personage than Prince Talleyrand. His distinguished son kept up, something of the family state, but, living much abroad, affairs fell into neglect. Cooper and Professor Morse, the inventor of the magnetic telegraph, were intimate friends. They knew each other as young men, when Cooper was a literary fledgling and Morse an obscure artist at Cooperstown; they knew each other in Europe, when each had become famous. After his death,* the

* J. Fenimore Cooper died Sept. 14th, 1851, aged sixty-two years.

family was broken up, and the Cooper mansion, after various vicissitudes, was finally burned. The obliteration of such an historical landmark is now regarded as a public loss. A son of the novelist is a lawyer at Albany —a most estimable gentleman, but of no literary ambition. One of the daughters is married to a wealthy gentleman in Cooperstown. Three other daughters are also residents of Cooperstown at the present time.

COOPER'S GRAVE AND MONUMENT.

"Cooper sleeps in the village cemetery beside his kindred, an unpretending slab marking the site of his grave. His monument is at the new cemetery, on the eastern shore of the lake, just beyond the site of the panther scene in the 'Pioneer.' It is of Italian marble, twenty-five feet high, with a figure of Leatherstocking on the summit. Natty is represented as loading his rifle and gazing off on the lake spread out beneath him, while his dog by his side watches his master with eager interest.

"The die is carved with symbols in *alto-rilievo:* on one side is the name of 'Fenimore Cooper,' surrounded by palm and oak branches; on the opposite is the student's lamp and inkstand, with the pen borne aloft by an eagle. On the north side are the naval emblems (Cooper served in the navy some time), and on the south the Indian devices—bow and quiver of arrows, scalp-locks on a lance, tomahawk, and necklace of beavers' claws."

THE ANDRUSTOWN SETTLERS.

ALLUSION has already been made to the ancient
" German Settlement," in the north part of the town of
Warren, known as " Andrustown." One cannot but
contemplate with interest this little colony of seven
families, subsisting through many years upon the small
area of land from which they had cleared away the forest,
the dark primeval wilderness shutting them in on all
sides. Let it be borne in mind that we write of a period
long before the Revolution; anterior even to the " Old
French War," before the adventurous New-Englander had
turned his attention to the wild solitudes of Central New
York. For the Andrustown colonists the nearest point
of civilization was the German settlement at Herkimer
(then German Flats), nine miles distant, and only accessible by an Indian path.

From the hostile incursions of the French and their
barbarous allies, the savages, these settlers were in constant danger; and when, in 1756 and 1757, these enemies
overran and devastated the " German Flats," the Andrustown colonists shared the dangers and sufferings of their
countrymen in the valley. A letter published in the
" *New York Mercury*," of May 22d, 1758, being a
relation of the murder committed at the " German Flats,"
near " Fort *Herchamer*," by " 80 Indians, and 4 Frenchmen," states as follows: " About 3 o'clock, most part of
the inhabitants, having notice from *Captain Herchamer*,
left their homes, and assembled at the Fort. Four families, that fled from Henderson's purchase (Andrustown)
in the spring for fear of the enemy, could not get in, and
had in their houses two Indian traders, of the name of
Clock, and six wagoners that were carrying Captain Gage's

baggage to the Fort. At 4 o'clock, all of a sudden, the houses were attacked; and the wagoners, being surprised, ran up stairs the better to defend themselves. The Indians immediately rushed into the house and killed and scalped all that were below; some of the Indians attempted the stairs, but were knocked down by the wagoners; they then fired up through the loft, and soon were joined by more Indians, who fired many shots quite through the house, and proposed to set it on fire, which intimidated John Ehel, a wagoner, to such a degree, that he leaped out at a window, thinking to make his escape, but was soon killed. The other five defended themselves with great intrepidity, having killed one Indian, until they were relieved by a party of rangers who came to their assistance; and after exchanging a few shots, the Indians fled, seeing our people having the advantage of a log-fence." We have given the above extract, only to show the participation of the "Andrustown" colonists. Could they be collected into a volume, it would form a story of thrilling and patriotic interest. The names of the seven families forming the colony were Hoyers, Starring, Osterhout, Crims, *Bell*. Descendants of all these families are still living, and in some instances upon the sites originally chosen by their ancestors. George Henry *Bell*, a member of the Andrustown family of that name, married Catherine, the sister of General Herkimer, and participated in the sanguinary battle of "*Oriskany*." Referring to him Mr. Benton, in his history of *Herkimer* County, says: "Although not among the militia officers appointed in 1775, he (Bell) commanded a company at the Oriskany battle, was wounded there, and afterwards placed on the invalid pension-roll. His disability continued through life. Captain Bell remained on the battle-field with *General*

Herkimer," until the action was over, and took charge of the escort which carried his wounded commander more than thirty miles on a litter. He brought with him from Oriskany a gun which he took in a hand-to-hand fight with a British officer, whom he killed. This trophy was long retained in the family, and exhibited as evidence of military prowess. George Bell, Esq., of Jordonville, is a descendant of this family. (*D. J. Crain.*)

The first liberty pole erected in the Mohawk Valley was at the German Flats, in 1775, and was cut down the same year by British authority. The first settlement of Andrustown was made in the year 1722.

THE CRUGER MANSION,

KNOWN as the " Henderson Home," was erected in the year 1836, at a cost of thirty thousand dollars. It is an ancient-looking stone structure, situated at an elevated point, in the extreme northern part of the town of Warren, Herkimer County, overlooking the deep valley of the Mohawk River. It is seven miles directly north from Richfield Springs. The estate on which this mansion stands was originally granted to Dr. Henderson, a surgeon in the royal army of Great Britain, and consisted of twenty-six thousand acres. Mrs. Harriet Cruger inherited fifteen hundred acres of the estate, and built the mansion that bears her name. Mrs. Cruger was descended from the famous Douglas family of Scotland. Was born June 29th, 1793; died May 5th, 1872.

JORDONVILLE.

This pleasant and sequestered little village is situated five miles to the north of Richfield Springs. It was first located by Hon. Jonas Cleland, in 1788. It is a neat thrifty hamlet, containing a population of 350 souls. Surrounded by a rich farming people, it is the centre of a profitable business, represented by one store, tailor and cabinet shop, two shoe stores and two blacksmith shops. Has one Baptist church, organized in 1799. The land on which the church stands, together with the cemetery ground, was donated by Eber Hyde; present pastor, Rev. Peter Goo. One Methodist church; present pastor, Rev. D. O. Edgerton. A Reformed Dutch church, one and a half miles northeast of Jordonville, was organized in 1831; present pastor, Rev. J. M. Compton.

AROUND THE LAKE.

Among the diversity of popular drives and points of interest to the pleasure-seeker, we desire to call especial attention to the drive around the lake, a distance of twelve miles. Leaving the village, we pass to the west shore, about one mile distant, the road leading near the bank, but sufficiently elevated to give a commanding view of the entire surface of this, the beautiful Canadarago.

What a world of beauty, what delightful associations of history and romance, what charming scenery and bounding health is suggested by the name, made memorable in Indian tradition, and famous for its spring-born waters. Its broad surface, now smooth as a mirror, reflecting the distant mountains, now rippling to the touch of the cool breath of the neighboring forests, that rolls its tiny white-capped waves along the gravelly shores, and tosses the flotilla of row-boats like feathers; its picturesque little island, and all the changing scenery that greets us as we pass along its margin. We pass through a rich district of highly cultivated farms, with numerous cottages embowered in beautiful groves, and surrounded by fertile fields of luxuriant vegetation. Clear running brooks water the meadows and come laughing through green pastures that stretch far up the steep sides of forest-capped hills or mountains that border the lake on the west. We now enter the quiet little village of "Schuyler's Lake," with its rich pastoral surroundings. Turning to the eastward from this place, we pass over a pleasant road leading directly to the base of the high range of mountains that skirt the valley on the east. We cross the "Oaks Creek," at a point where occurred the adventures with the Indians previously noticed, and turning a graceful angle, we soon arrive at a point known as "Perkins' Hill."

Here we catch the most charming view of the lake, with its wood-covered island standing boldly out of the water, while the distant outlines of the receding hills seem to melt into the soft blue horizon beyond.

The road along this side of the lake is peculiarly pleasant, there being sufficient space lying between the lake and steep mountain declivities for open fields, between which the road passes. The banks, on the east side especially, abound in eligible sites for country residences, being high, and sloping gradually to the water's edge.

Few persons visit this place without acknowledging the beauties of the lake scenery of this region of country. The ranges of mountains with summits of different heights and shapes, the hills and plains, the waving curves which appear on the face of every landscape, the dark hues of the forest, the verdure of the fields, the towering cliffs, the rugged precipices, the dark glens and silent dells, the rills, rivers, and placid lakes, all combine to render this region beautiful, sublime, and picturesque, and a most charming resort for those who seek the quiet pleasures of rural life, and the recuperating influences of the mountain regions.

ADJOINING TOWNS.

SPRINGFIELD.

This town is situated directly to the east of Richfield. The first settlements in the town were made in 1762, at East Springfield, by John Kelley, Richard Ferguson, and James Young, from Ireland. Gustavus Klumph and Jacob Tygert came during the war. Mr. Tygert had two sons, John and Jacob, who were taken prisoners and carried to Canada during the Revolution. Soon after the war, Elisha Dodge, Col. Herrick, and Aaron Bigelow, from Connecticut, and Eli Parsons, Eliakim Sheldon, and Isaac White, from Massachusetts, settled in the central part of the town.

The first settlement in the town was destroyed by the Indians in 1778, as previously noticed. It has several flourishing villages, and also several mineral springs. There are four churches, viz.:

1st Presbyterian, Rev. T. F. Sanborne, pastor.

1st Methodist, Rev. L. P. Marvin, pastor.

1st Baptist, Rev. S. J. Douglass, pastor.

1st Universalist.

The northern part of Otsego Lake lies within the

bounds of this town. At the head of this beautiful lake is the princely mansion of Mr. *George Clark*, the son of an English nobleman, who settled at this place about the commencement of the present century. Mr. Clark is probably the most extensive *landholder* in the State of New York.

The oldest tombstone in the cemetery is inscribed "Elisha Dodge, 1794." Among the oldest citizens of the town are—

Mrs. Lucy Burnham,	. .	aged 95
Mrs. Barringer,	. . .	" 98
Mrs. House,	. . .	" 98

A correspondent of the "Otsego Republican" says, "There are now living in one school district in the town of Springfield, near the shore of Otsego Lake, the following ten persons, whose united ages aggregate 764 years, being an average of 76 years each, viz. :

William Thayer,*	.	. aged 80 years.	
Mrs. William Thayer,	.	" 75	"
Andrew Gilchrist,	.	. " 87	"
Linus Thurston,	.	. " 78	"
Mrs. Lyman White, .	.	" 78	"
Horace Coleman,	.	. " 76	"
Mrs. Hoke,	. .	. " 74	"
Miss Thurston,	.	. " 76	"
Aaron Peck,	. .	. " 70	"
Mrs. John Weir,	.	. " 70	"

John I. Casler and wife, of *Springfield Centre*, expect to celebrate their 62d "*wedding-day*" on the 5th of July next (1874). Being now "*only*" eighty years of age respectively, and at that period of life when they can

* Wounded at the Battle of "Lundy's Lane," in the last war with Great Britain;" was a soldier under Gen. Winfield Scott.

retire from more active pursuits, they confidently look forward to many peaceful years of connubial bliss and social enjoyment.

REV. ANDREW OLIVER.*

(From Annals of the American Pulpit.)

Andrew Oliver was born in the parish of Abbots-rule, Roxburghshire, Scotland, on the 31st day of January, 1762. His father, George Oliver, of English descent, led the humble life of a shepherd. His mother, Helen Freeman, who was Mr. Oliver's second wife, was a woman of eminent piety. They had four children, of whom Andrew was the youngest. He attended for a season a classical school in the North of England, and it is said that he was engaged for a time in learning the printer's business. He was so young when he became a subject of divine grace, that he could not remember the date of his conversion. At the age of fourteen he was received into the church. When twenty-four years old, he married Elizabeth, daughter of Robert Ormiston, a substantial farmer of Eckford, East Mains, Roxburgh-shire. Her mother's name was Mary Given. Shortly after his marriage, in 1786, he came over to this country. After residing two years at Saco, Maine, he removed to Londonderry, New Hampshire, where he became acquainted with the Rev. William Morrison, by whose influence he was led to prepare for the gospel ministry. He studied with Dr. Morrison, and applied himself to his work with so much assiduity and devotion that he became almost blind. After his licensure by the Presbytery of Londonderry in 1792, he undertook a missionary tour on horseback to the State of New York, taking with him,

* Grandfather of Mr. William Oliver, of this place.

on account of his blindness, a young man as guide. Though laboring under this great disadvantage, his preaching was very acceptable and edifying.

After his return, in 1793, he was called to take charge of the Presbyterian church in Pelham, Massachusetts. During his ministry in this place he enjoyed the society of the neighboring ministers, and was an intimate friend of the Rev. Samuel Taggart of Colerain, and Dr. Parsons of Amherst. * * * Leaving his family at Pelham, he set out in search of a new home, and extended his inquiries into the State of New York, where several years before he had labored for a time as a missionary. He spent several months in Springfield, Otsego County, New York. His services were so acceptable to the people of this place that they invited him to become their pastor. He accepted the call, and having made arrangements for his settlement, went back after his family. This consisted then of his wife and seven children, all of whom except the oldest were born at Pelham. When Mr. Oliver came to Springfield in 1806, there was no Presbyterian house of worship. He preached in the Baptist church on the hill at West Springfield, and also for a season half the time at Middlefield in a barn. After about nine months he purchased a small farm at East Springfield, and built a commodious house, with money that was due to him from Pelham. His son William, then a boy fourteen years old, went after it on horseback, bringing the money home in his belt. Feeling the necessity of a house of worship, he urged the people to undertake the work of erecting one. When the frame was up, and the completion of the work was delayed, in order to arouse their zeal in the enterprise, he preached an earnest and stirring sermon on Haggai i. 4 : " Is it time for you, O ye, to dwell in your ceiled houses, and this house lie waste ? " He contributed of his own limited means to this undertaking, and encouraged the people until the work was *finished*. During Mr. Oliver's residence in Otsego County, he enjoyed the society and friendship of the Rev. Dr. William Neill, then of Albany, and the Rev. John Smith, of Cooperstown; Dr. James Carnahan, of Utica; Rev. Eli F. Cooley, of Cherry Valley; Rev. Daniel Nash, of the Episcopal church, and others, by each of whom he was highly esteemed. He was instrumental with others in forming the Otsego County Bible Society, which was organized March 7th, 1813. The Rev. Daniel Nash, of Exeter, was the first president, and Mr. Oliver the first vice-president. In 1816 this society appointed him, together with the Rev. E. F. Cooley, of Cherry Valley, and James Fenimore Cooper, of Cooperstown, delegates to co-operate with others in forming the "American Bible Society." He died March 24th, 1833.

OTSEGO.

This town bounds Richfield on the south, and is noted as being the home of the renowned James Fenimore Cooper, the great American novelist. Cooperstown, the county seat, is in this township, and is the largest and most beautiful village in Otsego County. The first white man that ever trod the soil of this town was Cadwallader Colden,* previous to the French War. The first deaths in this town were those of two deserting soldiers, who were shot by order of General Clinton, in 1779, before the settlements were commenced. The Hon. John A. Dix, present Governor of the State, was once a resident of Cooperstown. Says Mr. Liver-

* Cadwallader Colden, President of his Majesty's (George II.) Council, and "Commander-in-Chief of the Province of New York, and its dependencies in America." (*Land Papers*, vol. xvi.)

more, "He purchased 'Apple Hill' of the heirs of R. Fenimore Cooper, in 1828, but sold it to Levi C. Turner at his removal to Albany, on his being appointed Adjutant General," etc.

EXETER.

This town lies on the west side of Canadarago Lake; the surface is hilly and broken, consisting mainly of elevated uplands. "Among the first settlers of this town were William Angel, Asahel Williams, Hagar Curtis, Joshua and Caleb Angel, Seth Tubbs, Bethel Martin (the two last in the west part of the town), and T. Brooks and M. Cushman on the Rockdunga." William Lidell emigrated from England and settled near Canadarago Lake soon after the Revolution. His two sons, Allen and Jonas Lidell, now occupy farms originally purchased by their father, William Lidell. This township is noted for its fine quality of butter and cheese. It has three villages, viz. West Exeter, Exeter Centre, and Schuyler's Lake village.* The last named has already been noticed. Exeter is purely an agricultural town.

WINFIELD,† HERKIMER COUNTY.

Mr. Benton says, "This town was settled by the whites before 1800. * * * A small part of it lay within

---

* Of the oldest citizens now living at the village of Schuyler's Lake, we may mention Ira Palmer and John Durfy.

† Named from General Winfield Scott. The first settlement was commenced in 1792. Among the early settlers were Jos. Walker, Timothy Walker, Captain Nathan Brown, Oliver Harwood, Oliver Corbit, Benjamin Cole, and Deacon Gile, from Massachusetts. Abel Brace came in from Connecticut in 1793. Josiah Harwood taught the first school, in 1794; Charles Brace kept the first inn, in 1794; John Dillingham the first store, in 1796.

the limits of the Old England district until the municipal organization of the counties in this part of the State into townships took place. * * * The village of West Winfield, whose population is nearly five hundred, is located very near the west bounds of Herkimer County. It contains an academy incorporated by the Regents of the University. A bank, organized under the laws of the State, has recently been established in this village."

The Richfield branch of the Delaware, Lackawanna and Western Railroad passes through the town of Winfield.

COLUMBIA, HERKIMER COUNTY.

Says Benton, "This town was settled before the Revolution, by several German families from the Mohawk River." The heads of the families who made one of the settlements were Conrad Orendorf, Conrad Frank, Conrad Fulmer, Frederick Christman, Timothy Frank, Nicholas Lighthall, Joseph Moyer, and Henry Frink. The place where these families were seated was known as "Coonrodstown," before Columbia was organized, in 1812, and is so noted to this day.

A few Germans had also seated themselves at a place then and since called Elizabethtown, to commemorate the name of one or more German matrons among the settlers. Columbia is purely an agricultural town. "Asahel Alfred settled in this town in 1791. He was a native of Connecticut, a farmer, and an honest man, of steady industrious habits and good morals. Was a soldier of the Revolution, having entered the service of his country in his fifteenth year, and served more than three years. He was in the battle of Monmouth; taken prisoner at the Cedars, in Canada, after a smart conflict between the Americans and a party of the enemy, consisting of whites and Indians, and, as usual in such cases, both parties took their covers of stumps and trees. Alfred was fired at by an Indian, but not hit. A second shot was made at him, and the ball struck the stump behind which he stood. Mr. Alfred discovered the Indian's head exposed while loading the third time, took deliberate aim at him, fired, and was not again molested from that quarter.

" The Americans were outnumbered, and made prisoners, and as soon as they surrendered, the Indians stripped them of all their clothing except their shirts and pantaloons. They took his hat, coat, vest, neckerchief, and silver knee and shoe buckles.

"When on the march to the British post, one of Mr. Alfred's fellow-prisoners, being feeble and not able to keep up with the rest, fell behind, and Alfred remained with him to help him along. While making their way as well as they could, an Indian came up, and putting the muzzle of his gun close to the sick man's head, blew out his brains. Mr. Alfred was not slow to overtake his fellow-prisoners. He was at the capture of Burgoyne and the British army. He died in June, 1853, aged ninety-three years, having always resided on the same farm on which he first located, and which was occupied by his son, Cyrus, in the old age of his father."

WARREN.

The leading events of this town have been given in another part of this work, viz. Andrustown, Jordonville, etc.

RICHFIELD MINERAL WATERS.

BY N. GETMAN, M.D.

THE value of all medicinal agencies is estimated according to their respective power in arresting the progress of the ravages of disease.

The use of mineral waters as a specific for diseases, dates back many centuries. The Greeks, who were, in the knowledge of medicine, far in advance of their predecessors, regarded medicated waters as a special boon from heaven, piously dedicating them to their god Hercules, because of their invigorating qualities. In Italy as well as in all the Roman dominions, they were a very common remedy. And, so great was the favor in which these fountains were held, ornamental edifices were erected over them, and placed under a tutelary god. But beyond the general or special benefit experienced, unassisted by the light which modern chemical analysis sheds, they knew nothing. Not so with the medical practitioner of to-day. So well are the various diseases defined, and their specifics understood, that relief may be realized in any and all cases not beyond the reach of appropriate remedies. Many years since, blood-letting and heavy drastic doses of medicine went out of use; and a more humane, successful practice was adopted. For touch lightly the handiwork of God, as seen in the almost infinitely delicate machinery of the human body, is now the study of the best medical talent of the land. To this work, in this way, mineral waters hold a high place.

The delicate commingling of healing and curative properties, the precise amount of each being well understood, renders them a mild, safe, and efficient remedy. And yet it has not been found either wise or safe to use them without the advice which physicians well versed in their application can give.

In a practice of seventeen years, I have given much time and attention to the nature and application of the " mineral" waters of this place, in the treatment of the various diseases that afflict mankind. Their efficacy in chronic diseases has been most thoroughly and satisfactorily tested. In many cases, my first work has been to remedy the mischief of a too hasty and unwise use of the waters. For all must concede that even mild remedies, taken at improper times, and in immoderate quantities, into a system unprepared, may aggravate old diseases, if they do not create new ones. These views being the result of the observations of the medical faculty generally, it follows that "*experience*" is the only safe guide in the application of these waters.

While the physician can, and does know the properties of the "mineral waters," nothing but a careful diagnosis of the special cases to be treated can enable him judiciously to administer them in these cases. Of ten persons afflicted with dyspepsia, no two may require the same treatment, because of the hidden causes being so diverse. Recent cases of disease may and do find speedy relief. Others require more time, extending to one, two, or even three years, before a complete cure has been effected.

Some of these cases I shall refer to, illustrating the varied action and time of these waters as applied to the variety of persons and diseases presented for treatment. But it will not accord with the brevity of this treatise to multiply the recital of these cases. I shall therefore content myself with a brief reference to a few of the many persons who have sought and found relief at these fountains of *health*, where the benign "goddess Hygeia" presides. The Sulphur Spring waters, presenting the greatest claim for valuable medical properties, and ranking equally with any and all others upon this continent, and outranking even the celebrated Harrowgate Springs of England, are especially valuable in the treatment of the following diseases, viz. : rheumatism, neuralgia, psoriasis, cutaneous diseases, acne, eczema, erysipelas, erythema, herpes, porrigo, tinea or scald-head, secondary syphilis, scrofula, constipation, piles.

RHEUMATISM.

This painful disease is no respecter of persons. It assails alike the young, the middle-aged, and the aged, adhering with the greater tenacity to the last named ; but whether in a chronic or more recent form, yields readily to the judicious application of these waters. Induced by causes about as various and numerous as the patients affected, a correct understanding of each case becomes a necessity in order that the full benefit of the waters may be received. The warm bath, in connection with the internal use of these waters, has never yet failed to alleviate or cure when used in accordance with competent advice and reasonable perseverance. This point needs to be *especially* impressed upon the patient. The approaches of disease in these chronic cases have been so insidious that, in many, a term of years has elapsed before their distinct development. The lesson of this fact should impress upon the patient's mind the absolute necessity of "*time*" in which nature can, under the assisting, healing forces, work off her old and diseased parts, and assert herself in a new and healthy form. A

most marked case of speedy relief was enjoyed by a gentleman, some three years since, from England. Being
entirely helpless, he was carried by the sailors, from the
dock in Liverpool, on board the steamship, which in due
time landed him in New York, where, by similar agencies, he was carried from the ship to the coach which
placed him upon the train that landed him in Richfield.
The reader will readily understand that rheumatism
had deprived him of the power of locomotion. In less
than four weeks from Liverpool, he was walking about
this village, and taking his baths unassisted, except by
his cane. This case was undoubtedly an exceptional
one, on any other hypothesis than that his disease was
of but recent origin.

A very severe case of chronic rheumatism was a
Mrs. M——, aged fifty-five years, who was brought here
in 1867. Her disease was "*articular*," with more or less
muscular deformity, and utterly powerless to move or
help herself. Was carried to the baths, of which she was
able to take only six the first season, and attended with but
slight improvement. Drank the waters during the following winter, and returned in the spring of 1868, with
marked improvement, walking with the aid of crutches.
Was able to increase the baths to two a week during
this season, and returned home able to walk without
crutches. Came again in the spring of 1869, and at the
end of this season returned home with greatly improved
health. In 1873 she spent the season with an invalid
friend, so thoroughly well as to occupy the fourth floor at
the Spring House, during her stay here.

Mrs. F——, aged thirty-five years, came here in 1867
with a most aggravated case of eczema, the whole surface
of the body diseased, unable to see any one except her
attendant, receiving her meals in her room, and going to

the baths closely veiled. The second season she was cured. Visited these Springs in 1872, entirely free from her old complaint.

THE MAGNESIA SPRING.

This fountain is located just to the north of the large sulphur spring. Has for many years been known to contain important and useful medical properties, amounting to specifics in the cure of the following special diseases and their kindred ailments:

Dyspepsia, gastralgia, water-brash, chronic gastritis, diseases of the liver, chronic diarrhœa, diseases of the urinary organs, diabetes, catarrh of the bladder, Bright's disease of the kidneys, and the correlative diseases.

The same general rules to be observed by the patient laid down for the other springs applies also to this. The freedom with which these mineral waters can be obtained, should not tempt the patient to an excessive use of them.

CASE.—Mr. E——, aged fifty years, a lawyer, from Utica, visited these springs fourteen years ago, and not getting the relief anticipated from the sulphur spring, had recourse to the magnesia water, with such satisfactory results that he enthusiastically urges his dyspeptic friends to commence the use of these waters.

CHRONIC DIARRHŒA.

CASE.—Mr. S——, aged fifty-six years, came here in reduced flesh, having been afflicted with this disease for three years. Commenced with small doses three times a day. Gradually improved, with restored strength and edacity the first season. Took no baths.

THE CHALYBEATE WATER.

This spring is known to possess remarkable tonic properties, found to be useful in a great variety of female diseases and general debility. They have proved useful in the treatment of amenorrhœa, dismenorrhœa, chlorosis, leucorrhœa, ulceration of the uterus, and all nervous diseases. The restorative power of the "mineral waters" of Richfield have been abundantly demonstrated under my personal observation.

RICHFIELD MINERAL WATERS.

BY W. B. CRAIN, M.D.

Doctor W. T. Bailey:

Dear Sir:—I thank you for your unmerited consideration in requesting of me an article on the use of the " mineral waters " of Richfield. Their increasing importance magnifies the compliment, inasmuch as for that reason even what I shall write will be the more likely to be read, like the other portions of your undoubtedly interesting work. The earnest pursuit of my profession for some years in this vicinity, has not only impelled me to some acquaintance with the medicinal properties of the waters, but has also inspired me with something like a local patriotism, and a high opinion of its mere *locality* for *healthful* and sanitary purposes. In considering the merits of various " watering-places," we are not to confine ourselves to the *waters* alone. If this were so, the waters of *Baden Baden* or *Saratoga* might just as well be used at home. To represent the *hygienic* claims of this or that locality, by a bottle of their waters, would be like the man who, having a farm to sell, carried about in his pocket a little box of the *soil* as a specimen. To some extent it may be a caprice of mine—but repeated observation has convinced me that Richfield and vicinity have some *other* sanitary claims by no means to be disregarded. I see them through their unusually clear and bracing atmosphere. I see them in their deep, rich, and thoroughly wholesome soil—in the longevity bespoken by their living, and written on the tombstones of their dead. The old buried * centenarian of the "Boston Tea-party" furnishes an example.

It is also of some consequence in connection with health, that a watering-place should be ample in its natural incentives and provisions for out-door exercises, employments, and pleasures; and what locality can be more so than that of Richfield? The attractiveness of its drives, rides, and rambles—its fishing, boating, and pleasure parties, and the beauty and magnificence of its surrounding scenery, are now almost proverbial. The body is invigorated together with the soul. The blood tingles as the lungs imbibe the cool dry air, and the eyes feast upon the splendid prospects of nature. To this we may add that the place, once so difficult of access, is now easy by rail, with ample comforts on arrival. A few years since the charge of "too full" was justly made; and when the guest complained of his *coffee*, he perhaps had "*grounds.*" But not so now. All that fine hotels or cosey lodgings can do for the "creature comforts" of the invalid are full and complete.

It is a great mistake to suppose that mineral waters, and what are now known as "watering-places," are at all modern in their celebrity. They were well known to the Greeks and Romans, and have been more or less so through all the ages since. Galen, Hippocrates, and many others of their time were well acquainted with their hygienic value, and applied them systematically to the cure of diseases. The Romans, "prompted by gratitude for

* G. R. T. Hewes, aged 109 years.

the benefits which they derived from them, decorated their sites with edifices." In 1670 the mineral waters of France were first analyzed by a commission of the Academy of Sciences, and from that time to the present the use of such remedies has been steadily increasing, as well as the public confidence in their efficacy. The best known mineral waters are now prescribed by the medical faculty in certain cases with as much confidence as any preparation of the apothecary. Mineral waters are generally divided into four varieties, viz. acidulous, chalybeate, saline, and sulphurous; to the latter of which mostly belong those of Richfield. This was the variety patronized largely by the *luxurious* Romans, however disagreeable their odors may prove to modern nostrils.

With all that chemical learning has done in the analysis of mineral waters (and there is yet much undone), their real stamp of value is involved, simply, in what experience has decided as to their *efficacy*. If it be true that most of the mineral waters longest used and best known have never been *thoroughly* analyzed, the same is doubly true of the waters of Richfield; but it is equally true that within the comparatively brief time that has elapsed since they became at all extensively known, their curative powers have proven very remarkable. With all that has been written in Europe and America on the subject of mineral waters, it is perhaps not very surprising that nothing has yet appeared doing any justice to the waters of Richfield. The celebrity they have earned in spite of this fact, is the best proof of their real worth. But the time is certainly come when something should be written of which the little I shall say is a mere prelude. There should be a work of some kind, embodying a guide to the use of these waters, and enabling those who employ them to do it with intelligence. It is not

my design to prescribe rules for their use in obscure and
intricate cases—as any one at all familiar with the vari·
ous forms of disease would at once recognize its im-
practicability ; but *general* rules may with propriety be
stated. I am indebted to Drs. Bell, Moorman, Armstrong, and others, for many valuable ideas, and have
freely consulted their works in the preparation of this
letter.

As a rule, no preparatory treatment is required before
commencing the use of the waters. Plethoric subjects
with a naturally sluggish liver, who suffer from undue
determination of blood to the brain, may with advantage
anticipate their use by a mild purgative ; but the necessity for powerful cathartics seldom exists. Cold water
may be most safely indulged in during the early part
of the day, when the body is in its "greatest vigor."
Toward evening it is less able to resist strong impressions.
Hence a full glass of the water one hour before breakfast, and a second glass thirty minutes later, may be taken
with impunity by the majority of persons, and perhaps
with more benefit than at any other hour of the day.
A third glass may be taken one hour before dining, and a
fourth before tea. Large draughts are hurtful, and it is
unnecessary to gorge the stomach with mineral waters
in order to obtain their remedial effects. It must be
admitted that there are those who take enormously large
quantities for many consecutive days without apparent
inconvenience or injury, and come to the "Springs" with
the conviction that the sooner they can "*saturate*" their
systems, the more rapidly will their ailments disappear.
Not only is this theory untenable, but flooding the
stomach with large and continued potations of water
may not only produce serious derangement of the
digestive organs, but engender such repugnance to the

waters as to thwart the sole object in coming to the Springs. Dr. Bell remarks that " water drunk to excess distends the stomach, dilutes to extreme tenuity the gastric juice, diminishes the vital energy of the gastric mucous membrane. Nausea, flatulence, oppression at the pit of the stomach, colics, diarrhœa, aqueous plethora of the vascular system, weakness of the nervous centres, pallor, and aversion to locomotion, may all follow in the train of excessive potations of water." Mineral waters are confessedly powerful stimulants to the glandular system, and their alterative effect can in no way be so surely obtained as by taking moderate quantities at suitable hours. Inordinate draughts simply excite the kidneys and bowels to undue action, and are consequently not retained in the system sufficiently long to produce their alterative influence. Like all remedies of equal potency, they should be taken guardedly at first, and the quantity increased as tolerance is manifest and the nature of the malady seems to demand. Too much caution cannot be observed by those who suffer from debility of the digestive organs—especially females whose nervous systems have been prostrated by chronic diseases, and who so constantly suffer from gastralgia and the kindred disorders of the digestion apparatus. Such patients, however, may derive lasting benefit from the waters taken with moderation. The more serious the derangements of the digestive organs the greater should be the caution in using them. The magnesia water is well adapted to cases of enfeebled digestion as experience has shown; but even it should be allowed to stand in an open vessel sufficiently long for the *gas* to escape before it is taken. Those who have a lymphatic constitution, who are feeble and infirm, and who suffer from a morbid sensibility of the mucous surfaces, may with propriety take the waters before rising, and they may with benefit anticipate their use by some mild and nourishing drink —a part of a cup of broma answering a very good purpose.

Elderly persons suffering from chronic urinary disease should never attempt the use of the waters until they have sought advice. Giddiness and the unpleasant feeling of constriction about the forehead *sometimes* experienced after taking the waters, may usually be prevented by drinking them two hours after instead of before meals. Mineral waters or cold drinks of any kind should never be indulged in immediately before or immediately after taking food. The stomach is then occupied with the digestive process, and any interruption is likely to be followed by not only temporary inconvenience, but permanent stomachic derangement. Upon the nature and duration of the disease, and the susceptibilities of the system to remedial agents, will depend the length of time it will be necessary to use the waters before the desired effect is produced. For many constitutions a *three weeks'* course is sufficient, while others require to take the waters during a period of *six* weeks or more before experiencing a decided impression. Dr. Moorman, in his most valuable treatise on mineral waters, in speaking of the White Sulphur of Virginia, says: "In some cases, where the system is previously well prepared, and the subsequent management judicious, the White Sulphur will produce its alterative operations in about two weeks: such cases, however, are rare, and it will generally be found that from *three* to *six* weeks or even longer must elapse under its use before those *profound* changes are wrought which precede and insure a return to health." These remarks, so far as they relate to time, are applicable to all our mineral waters that remove disease by virtue of their *alterative* action. It is not unusual to hear persons remark that they experienced no benefit from the waters while at the *Springs*, but felt themselves improved after returning to their homes. The same good results would doubtless have been manifest had they remained at the resort sufficiently long to observe the " sanative " effect. Similar experience attends the use of all alterative remedies; and if we based our ideas of the value of mineral waters upon their *sensible* effects alone, such as increased intestinal and renal action, we should often be discouraged in the very onset.

Perhaps no marked change will be noticed in the action of any organ while using the waters, yet the quiet work of restoring a healthy tone to the glandular system may commence when the first glass is taken: should the powerful *diuretic* and *cathartic* action so usually looked for not follow the use of the waters, the patient need not be disheartened. A change in the character of the secretions and excretions is oftentimes of vastly more importance than a mere increase or diminution of either, and the work of restoring the economy to its normal integrity will take place under the use of the waters, though no increased action of the kidneys or bowels is observed.

In HEPATIC DERANGEMENTS the Richfield waters act with decided force; hence abdominal plethora, ascites, defective digestion, depression of spirits, etc., etc., resulting from a torpid condition of the liver, are usually promptly relieved. Constipation resulting from deficient biliary secretion or from atony of the muscular coat of the intestines is usually much benefited. In neuralgia, nervous debility, hysteria, and chorea, the invigorating influence of these waters, aided by the bracing air of the neighborhood, is at once observable. Nervous pains recurring in paroxysms and affecting different parts of the body, so commonly the result of a rheumatic or gouty diathesis, quickly disappear under the use of these waters.

In chronic inflammation of the kidneys, bladder, and urethra, when not dependent upon serious structural disease, a course of the baths combined with drinking the waters has in very many cases proven most beneficial. By chemically altering the quality of the blood the urine is rendered less irritating to the urinary passages, and hence the waters in this way prove serviceable in this class of diseases, besides acting powerfully as a diuretic.

In chronic rheumatic and gouty affections, the Richfield waters have a well-merited reputation. Dr. Fuller, in his treatise on Rheumatism, says of the use of mineral waters in this disease, "that when everything else fails, they not unfrequently afford extraordinary and permanent relief. Whatever the modus operandi of the waters, their free use both internally and externally exercises a beneficial influence *which is in vain* sought from medicine and bathing in *other* places. The effect produced is at once sedative and tonic. The pain-worn sufferer, irritable and anxious, repairs to the springs, unable to sleep and troubled with dyspepsia, connected with a sluggish condition of the skin, liver, kidneys, and bowels : after ten days' or a fortnight's trial of their virtues, he begins to find himself less irritable, less anxious, and less wakeful ; he sleeps more soundly, and feels more refreshed by his sleep; his digestion improves—the whole system is invigorated." Nor is this picture overdrawn. Sulphurous waters, when systematically and intelligently used, seldom fail to relax the rigidity of the muscular system, to reduce the enlargements and restore motion to diseased joints, and, by establishing a healthy action of all the emunctories, eradicate the materies morbi from the circulating fluids, which beget a rheumatic or gouty diathesis. Decided amelioration may be looked for even in confirmed gout. I have seen unsightly nodes, so often met with in this disease, materially lessened under a protracted use of these waters. They are not well adapted to the acute form of this disease.

In the treatment of dropsy we have in the Richfield waters a powerful adjuvant, amounting in many cases to almost a specific—acting with decided force upon the bowels, kidneys, and skin : when taken largely and with a view to promote an increased activity of these organs, many stubborn cases of ascites and general anasarca have yielded under their use.

Many of the skin affections so obstinate under the ordinary plans of treatment, are much benefited, if not entirely relieved, by a full course of the baths and waters. In chronic eczema, lepra, psoriasis, and acne, great relief may be expected. Dr. Armstrong remarks that " almost all cutaneous affections will yield more rapidly to the continued internal use of sulphurated hydrogen gas than to any of the means now commonly employed." Dr. Horace Manley, of this village, the first physician who systematically prescribed these waters, and who has observed their effect for about fifty years, speaks enthusiastically of their virtues in strumous diseases. Children suffering from indolent glandular tumors about the neck, from tumid abdomens the result of scrofulous disease of the mesenteric glands, thrive wonderfully under the use of these waters. Their salutary operation has also been noticed in chronic catarrh and in some of the chronic *bronchial* affections. The theory is often advanced that sulphurous waters and the atmosphere in the vicinity of sulphur springs are antagonistic to a healthy condition of lung tissue. This really has no foundation in fact. Considering the severity of our climate during the winter and spring months, it must be admitted that pulmonary diseases are comparatively rare in this immediate vicinity and surrounding country. Dr. Manley, whose opinion is supported by extended observation, remarks that "deaths from consumption are much less frequent in this locality now than they were forty years ago," and that he cannot recall a case of true tubercular disease that developed itself in any subject born and reared within the corporate limits of the village! I don't wish to be understood as recommending Richfield Spa as a particularly favorable resort for persons suffering from consumption, but I do assert that consumptive patients are as exempt while here from the exciting causes of the disease, and from the influences which tend to aggravate it when existing, as at any point of equal elevation. It too frequently happens that patients *far* advanced in consumption frequent resorts of this kind, either by the advice of physicians or friends. Their digestive powers being enfeebled by tubercular deposit, perhaps in the stomach and bowels, their vitality being lowered by exhausting discharges, discouraged in mind and disgusted with medicine, they select some watering-place as a last resort, and without competent advice they deluge their stomachs with mineral waters, and then further seek to refresh themselves by a warm or *hot* bath. A few who pursue this course may escape any serious aggravation of their systems, but the majority will add fuel to the fire that is slowly consuming them. I am confident much of the odium cast upon resorts like this arises from the unfortunate experiments of consumptive patients. Those who have incurred a predisposition to tubercular development by a too protracted residence in malarious districts, whose vitality has been lessened by confinement, whose glandular system has become torpid, may derive untold benefit from a summer's sojourn at Richfield. Dr. Armstrong, in speaking of the value of "Harrowgate" and "Dinsdale" waters (the virtues of which he admits depend in a great measure upon the sulphurated hydrogen gas which they contain), says: "A remedy so highly efficacious in chronic inflammation in general, might seem at first sight well fitted for phthisis and similar insidious affections; and though my experience is very incomplete with respect to its powers in confirmed consumption, yet it has seemed to me exceedingly useful in several instances where phthisis was distinctly threatened. But this has been more especially observable where the pectoral symptoms were complicated with hepatic disorder, as frequently occurs; and indeed in the commencement of most fevers of the hectic type the sulphurous waters have afforded more relief than anything else. In a few solitary cases which bore the characters of genuine and confirmed phthisis, and in which pus was expectorated, a marked change for the better took place from the drinking of the Dinsdale waters; and I recently saw two remarkable examples, which appeared to be cured by this mineral spring, though in both the disease was far advanced when it was first tried." In paralysis the waters are taken with various results; when not dependent upon serious organic lesions, much benefit usually follows their use. Persons suffering from venereal poison and its *sequelæ*, iritis, rheumatism, and troublesome cutaneous affections, usually find in these waters a complete antidote. Several patients have taken them with success after a protracted but fruitless sojourn at the Hot Springs of "Arkansas." In intermittent fever their good effects are soon appreciable. Those cases resulting from a long residence in unhealthy sections, that have worn out the ordinary remedies, convalesce rapidly after coming to this climate. In chronic ophthalmia, occurring in scrofulous subjects, much benefit may be anticipated.

In chronic enlargement of the spleen much relief is experienced after a full course of the baths and waters.

Latterly, Richfield has become quite a favorite rendezvous for persons suffering from "*hay asthma*." Whether the disease depends upon some peculiar exhalation, or, as Dr. Blackley asserts, upon the existence of pollen grains of various grasses intimately mixed with common dust, I will not pretend to argue; but experience abundantly establishes the fact that persons accustomed to annual visitations of this disease in other localities, are here wholly exempt. Among those who enjoy such exemption may be mentioned Com. W. N. Inmann, U. S. N.; Rev. E. M. Pecke, rector of St. John's Church in this village; Mrs. Colonel Willoughby, of Saratoga. Many others might be mentioned who hold Richfield in kind remembrance on account of the complete immunity it has afforded them from this most perplexing disease.

The value of these waters as an "*aphrodisiac*" has long been recognized, and they are now frequently prescribed in impotency with abundant success.

It will be observed that to chronic diseases the Richfield waters are more particularly adapted. They are inadmissible in acute inflammatory troubles, on account of their decided stimulating properties. Patients suffering from undue determination of blood to any of the important organs should take the waters with the utmost caution. Serious consequences may follow their use in organic disease of the heart and blood-vessels; also in pulmonary consumption when in its advanced stage. They are likewise contraindicated in gastro-intestinal inflammation :

in prostatic enlargement the waters do no good, and may, by flooding the bladder, do permanent injury. Should the bowels become constipated, the urine scanty, the tongue furred, the pulse rapid, under the use of the waters, it is better to discontinue them for a short time, and attempt to relieve the system by some mild aperient. With many persons the use of the waters gives rise to constipation in the commencement: this may usually be overcome by judiciously and gradually increasing the quantity; if not, its action may be aided by a glass of Congress water or Rochelle powder in the morning, or some mild pill after dining. It may generally be considered a favorable indication when patients take the waters with pleasure.

The warm sulphur baths are usually employed in aid of the waters taken internally; and besides accomplishing all that an ordinary warm bath does, they exert a particulary tonic influence. The temperature of the bath is important, and should be considered by all, especially invalids. A cool bath ranges from 60° to 75°; temperate bath, from 75° to 85°; a tepid bath, from 85° to 90°; warm bath, from 92° to 98°; a hot bath, from 98° to 112° *Fahrenheit*. The warm sulphur baths are mostly in vogue here, though bran and medicated baths are often prescribed. No more grateful and appropriate remedy can be prescribed for the fatigue incident to a long journey, when the skin is harsh and dry, the pulse irritable, the secretions scanty, than a warm bath. By allaying the irritability of the nervous system, refreshing sleep is almost always insured. The catalogue of diseases to which the baths are applicable is quite large, but I deem it sufficient to mention a few only, and those most frequently treated. It may be said that the bath is useful in most cases in which the water is admissible: hence in chronic rheumatism and gout, in chronic affections of the liver and spleen. By relieving the congestion of the gastro-enteric mucous membrane, they prove beneficial in chronic diarrhœa and dysentery ; in the same manner long-standing nephritic affections and diseases of the bladder are relieved. In many of the functional diseases of the womb, such as painful and deficient menstruation, chronic engorgement of the uterus, and the various difficulties attending the final suppression. Abdominal neuralgia, gastralgia, and nephritic colic are also successfully treated by the warm bath. I have watched with the greatest satisfaction the effects of the baths and water in a vast number of cases of *sciatica*. I cannot recall one that was not benefited, but very many that were entirely cured. No one who has observed the effect of mineral waters when used for bathing purposes, will doubt but that at a certain temperature they are taken up by the absorbents into the general circulation, and in this way exercise to some extent a remedial influence. Not only are the absorbing but the exhaling functions of the skin increased by the warm bath, and hence their special celebrity in most diseases of this organ. Acting as a detergent, the skin is thoroughly cleaned of its impurities, which might otherwise be reabsorbed, its texture is softened, and its natural functions fully restored. In diseases of this class the bran and medicated baths are often used with benefit.

The "hot bath" is a decidedly active agent, and should never be indulged in except when particularly advised. It is, in fact, a *powerful* stimulant, and instead of tranquilizing the circulation, etc., like the warm bath, it excites the heart to undue action : under its influence the skin becomes red, the pulse rapid, the respirations hurried, and the mind obtuse. After a time, profuse perspiration sets in, which is usually followed by decided languor and debility. Before breakfast is probably the most suitable time for bathing; but guests usually find it more convenient to bathe between the hours of 10 A. M. and 1 P. M. A hot or warm bath should never be indulged in while the stomach is occupied with the process of digestion; and a short time should always elapse after the bath, before taking food, in order that the mucous lining of the stomach may recover from the excitement incident to the bath. No good objection can be urged to the use of the bath immediately before retiring at night, especially when patients seek, in addition to the other good effects, the boon of refreshing sleep.

The duration of the bath will depend much upon the susceptibilities of the patient and the nature of the disease. As a rule it should not exceed fifteen or twenty minutes; but in some obstinate troubles, the immersion may be continued for an hour or more (in warm bath) with entire safety, and perhaps with better prospect of relief.

Should symptoms of vertigo and confusion of thought supervene upon the use of the baths, they may usually be relieved by the application of a towel saturated in cold water to the forehead. It is perhaps well for the inexperienced to use this as a preventive during the bath.

After coming from the bath, every patient should retire, and remain *comfortably* covered in bed for an hour at least, in order that the equilibrium of the circulation may be restored before the body is again exposed to atmospheric changes.

The matter of dress should be considered by all who desire to reap the full benefits of the baths and waters, and who expect to render comfortable their stay at Richfield.

The average temperature during the months of July and August does not vary much from eighty-five degrees during the day; but after sunset the thermometer often falls rapidly to sixty, and continues to indicate this low temperature during the entire night. While this is eminently conducive to sleep, persons not accustomed to such sudden transitions are very likely to suffer serious inconvenience from them. A suit that is adapted to the spring months in our northern climates should always be at hand; besides, a firm overcoat or shawl will often be found a most comfortable companion. Delicate persons, who are particularly susceptible to colds, who suffer from neuralgia or rheumatisim, should always wear woven silk or soft flannel wraps.

REGIMEN.—The less the stomach is harassed by indigestible and unwholesome food, the more readily will the waters be assimilated. It would be a very difficult matter to suggest the particular kind or quantity of food that should be taken by the *different* persons who come here from year to year, and a still more difficult matter to insist upon your suggestions being carried out. Inasmuch as the waters tend to stimulate the appetite, it is well for all to be guarded as to the quantity as well as the quality of food they take, selecting, from the variety presented them, that which is light and nourishing, and best adapted to their powers of digestion and assimilation. As a rule, the same good judgment that protects them from indiscretions in diet while using the more familiar remedies, will serve them during the use of mineral waters.

The old and infirm to whom *wine* has become a necessary of life, are not required to abstain from it while taking the waters. Those who are sufficiently strong to forego its use, especially rheumatic and gouty subjects, who can so often trace their sufferings to too free indulgence, would do well to abandon all stimulants.

Very truly yours,

WM. BAKER CRAIN, M.D.

RICHFIELD SPA, N. Y., *March* 18, 1874.

THE LAKE HOUSE.

W. H. LEWIS, PROPRIETOR.

THIS well-known and popular resort is located on the northeastern shore of Canadarago Lake, about one mile from the centre of the village. This house was erected in 1843, and has been devoted exclusively to the . entertainment of the guests of the Springs,* possessing every facility for fishing, hunting, and sailing on the lake, where a fleet of row and sail boats is always in *readiness.* A gravel-walk, beautifully shaded by large and gracefully sweeping willows, leads from the Lake House to the shore of the lake, where seats are provided, that invite us to while away the sultry hours, and inhale the freshening breezes that come wafting from the bosom of the rippling waters that glitter and dance in the rays of the midday sun. In the ravine to the left of the walk as we approach the lake, are the decaying trunks of several antiquated apple-trees, that were in their prime when first seen by the earliest settlers. They have since been known as the " Indian apple-trees." In the midst of the forest at the head of the lake is a large pool of " sulphur water," that has no doubt exhaled its sulphurous fumes to the forest air for unknown centuries.

* Lewis' sumptuous game dinners are no doubt remembered with pleasure by many who have partaken of them.

WALNUT-GROVE HOUSE.

WM. VAN CUREN, PROPRIETOR.

This house is situated two miles from the village of Richfield Springs, on the eastern shore of the lake, and directly opposite the island. The house is open through the boarding season for the entertainment of guests and pleasure-seekers, and is connected with the Springs by a regular line of *omnibuses*. The shore of the lake at this point is pleasantly shaded by large walnut-trees, and a fleet of row-boats kept for the pleasure of visitors. It is a very inviting resort.

SUMMER.

As health is more to be prized than silver and gold, and the heated term approaches, we turn away from the thronged streets of the large commercial towns and restless cities, to breathe the invigorating air of the mountains and valleys of the beautiful country. With what delightful emotions of freedom and pleasure do we greet the open and luxuriant fields, fragrant with wild flowers and sweet-scented clover, blooming fruit-trees, and variegated forests, filled with the music of birds that " sing among the branches," peacefully gliding rivers, rapidly flowing streams, leaping cascades, towering precipices, and cool umbrageous retreats, that invite us to their sylvan bowers! Wild and romantic lakes, with isolated islands, lovely cottages, and lordly mansions, are scattered throughout Central New York, and await the weary guests fleeing from the heated walls and impure streets of city life, to spend the summer days in cool retreats of luxury and repose. All the rhapsodies of the poets have never exaggerated the wonder and daily fascination of that miracle which annually transforms the bleak wintry landscape into the exuberance and beauty of summer.

Can any place be found more inviting to the stranger than the neat little village of Richfield Springs, with its almost boundless resources of health and pleasure, and varied attractions of summer luxuriance, with mountain and lake scenery that afford every facility for pleasure and healthful recreation ?

And now the delightful time has come, with " *the leafy month of June,*" and

" Summer is in the air, odors are everywhere ;
   Idle birds are singing loud and clear ;
  Brooks are bubbling over, heads of crimson clover
   On the edges of the field appear.

" All the meadow blazes with buttercups and daisies,
   And the very hedges are tangles of perfume ;
  Butterflies go brushing, all their plumage crushing,
   In among this wilderness of bloom.

" The thorn-flower bursts its sheath, the bramble hangs a wreath,
   And blue-eyed grasses beckon to the sun ;
  While gypsy pimpernel waits, eager to foretell
   When rainy clouds are gathering one by one.

" The very world is blushing, is carolling and gushing
   Its heart out in melody of song ;
  While simple weeds seem saying, in grateful transport praying,
   Unto Him our praises all belong."

10

THE GREAT RAIN-STORM.

THE Fourth of July, 1872, will long be remembered by the inhabitants of this place and surrounding country. The day opened bright and promising. By ten o'clock in the morning our streets were filled with eager eyes and anxious ears, watching the approach of a circus company entering the village from the west. The tent for this exhibition was located on the lowlands in the southern part of the village, near the railroad depot.

Soon the enlivening strains of the brass band of the circus company fell upon the ears of the merry thryng of young, middle-aged, and eager pilgrims who wended their way toward this, the great centre of attraction. Children danced gayly beside their more sedate ancestors, and everything "*went merry as a marriage-bell.*" Soon the immense tent was filled by a restless waiting crowd of over three thousand people, among which the guests of our numerous hotels were well represented.

The performance had already commenced, and immediately the sky was dark and portentous. Big drops of a frowning rain-cloud fell heavily on the rusty canvas over our unprotected heads. The writer found himself closely sandwiched between two sedate, adipose matrons, with whom he shared the temporary protection of a capacious cotton fabric.

> "Lord of the winds! I feel thee nigh
> I know thy breath in the burning sky!
> And I wait, with a thrill in every vein,
> For the coming of the hurried rain!
> It has come! do ye not behold
> The aqueous vapors, wet and cold,
> A whirling ocean that fills the wall
> Of the crystal heaven, and buries all?
> And I, cut off from the world, remain
> *Alone with the terrible hurricane.*"

The rain now fell in torrents, and came pouring through the canvas in every direction, irrespective of age, sex, or social position; and there was no exemption from the common baptism. Every expedient was resorted to by the *melancholy* audience for protection against the intrusions of this unwelcome humidity, but all was vain. We were now fully prepared to deeply sympathize with our antediluvian brethren, and still the rain continued as of old.

The ground was soon transformed into a miniature lake, and the low slippers and white stockings of an hour before, were concealed far beneath this turbulent compound of earth and water. Young men and maidens stood and gazed upon each other in sympathetic *silence*, earnestly contemplating the mystery of this relentless dispensation of *Providence*. And still it rained. With emotions of reluctance, many took refuge in waiting vehicles. Slowly and demurely they left this scene of disappointed hopes, and passed silently away to their respective destinations. Such a flood never was known before in Richfield. It impaired the roads and streets in every direction to such an extent that it required several months to repair them. As remarked by a gentleman at the time, "*This is* indeed a watering-place!"

"PICKING HOPS."

OTSEGO COUNTY is remarkable as being the great hop-producing county of the State; and almost every farm has several acres of the vine, that yield under ordinary circumstances an average of one thousand pounds to the acre. Hop-picking time is looked forward to with a good deal of interest, giving employment to hundreds of young ladies, who seem to delight in this annual festivity, as well as profitable occupation. Young men also being employed, connubial alliances are not unfrequently the result of these gatherings.

"PICKING HOPS."

BY ETHEL LYNN (1863).

On the hills of old Otsego,
　　By her brightly gleaming lake,
Where the sound of horn and hunter
　　Sylvan echoes love to wake,
Where the wreaths of twining verdure
　　Clamber to the saplings' tops,
I sat beside sweet Minnie Wilder,
　　In the great field, picking hops.

Then the clusters green and golden
　　Binding in her sunny hair,
Half afraid, yet very earnest,
　　Looking in her face so fair,
Speaking low, while Squire Von Lager
　　Talked of past and coming crops,
Said I, " Minnie, should a soldier
　　Stay at home here picking hops?

" While the country, torn asunder,
　　Calls for men like me to fight,
And the voice of patriots pleading
　　Ask for hands to guard the right ;
While from hearts of heroes slaughtered
　　Still the life-blood slowly drops,
Can I—shall I stay beside you,
　　Minnie, darling, picking hops ? "

Very pale the cheek was growing,
　　And the hand I held was cold ;
But the eye was bright and glowing,
　　While my troubled thought was told ;
Yet her voice was clear and steady,
　　Without sighs, or tears, or stops,
When she answered, speaking quickly,
　　" 'Tis women's work, this picking hops.

"Men should be where duty calls them,
Women stay at home and pray
For the gallant absent soldier,
Proud to know he would not stay."
"Bravely spoken, darling Minnie!"
Then I kissed her golden locks,
Breathed anew a soldier's promise,
As we sat there picking hops.

"Now I go away to-morrow,
And I'll dare to do or die,
Win a leader's straps and sword, love,
Or 'mid fallen heroes lie.
Then when all of earth is fading,
And the fluttering life-pulse stops,
Still, 'mid thoughts of home and heaven,
I'll remember picking hops."

ELK HORNS.

In the month of August, 1868, Mr. Ira Whiter, of the town of Warren, discovered two pairs of elk horns lying beneath the water near the shore of the lower lake, together with a quantity of bones, indicating the skeletons of two large elks. They had doubtless broken through the ice simultaneously while engaged in a fierce encounter. The partial decomposition of the antlers and bones, was sufficient proof that at least a century had passed since they were deposited there. A notice of these fossils appeared in one of the Albany journals, at the time of their discovery.

THE COMMON SCHOOL. (District No. 9.)

This district has a large and substantial building, that was erected in 1860, at a cost of three thousand dollars. There are about three hundred names in the district, that draw *public money*. This school has an average attendance of one hundred and fifty scholars, and has three terms annually of thirteen weeks each. There are two departments, primary and advanced. In the higher department, besides the common branches, the science of astronomy, philosophy, algebra, geometry, and vocal music, are taught.

Present teachers : Mr. E. D. Harrington, Miss Emma A. Getman.

PATENTS.

INVENTIONS RECENTLY PATENTED BY RESIDENTS OF RICHFIELD SPRINGS.

WALTER'S BURGLAR ALARM.

A VALUABLE INVENTION.

AMONG the practical and useful inventions of the age, we wish to call especial attention to a "burglar alarm," recently invented by Mr. H. E. Walter, of this place. We here present a cut of this little instrument, as it

appears when set up in working order. By the application of this alarm to any building, the inventor has secured the following great advantages over any other appliance. The alarm, which is invisibly connected with every exposed door and window in the house, is placed in the sleeping-room, and is operated by electricity. The simple turning of a button (or switch) on the alarm, is all that is necessary to connect or disconnect it with the windows or doors in any part of the house. When it is set for the night, the opening of any door or window in the building instantly rings the *bell*, which continues ringing until it is stopped by the person in charge. Closing them has no effect on the *alarm* to stop it after it is set in motion. A small pointer or indicator instantly tells you if a door or window is left open after you suppose them to be closed. The windows can be left open sufficiently for ventilation, and if moved either up or down, the bell instantly commences ringing, and at the same time, if the windows are closed, raising them one half inch causes the alarm to sound. When the alarm is set, it is impossible to remove a sash without ringing the bell.

Mr. Walter says, " We use a clock attachment when desired, which prevents the alarm ringing at any given hour in the morning. We set them up, on a closed circuit; by so doing we avoid the danger of a wire being cut or broken, or the battery becoming weak or entirely exhausted, without sounding the alarm. We use a new and exceedingly simple battery, made entirely of metal, which will last from eight to ten months, without any attention whatever." This alarm, when once set, requires no further attention, there being nothing to adjust.

THE WALTER ELECTRIC BURGLAR ALARM COMPANY was duly incorporated, January 24th, 1874, with a capital stock of $10,000. HORACE E. WALTER, President, A. R. ELWOOD, Secretary and Treasurer. First Board of Trustees: H. E. Walter, H. C. Walter, A. R. Elwood, A. H.

Elwood, and A. S. Howe. Place of business, Walter's Block, Richfield Springs, N. Y. General office and show-room, 13 and 14 Parker Block, Utica, N. Y.

1st. BOWDISH'S PHOTOGRAPH POSING CHAIR,

PATENTED in 1871. This chair is being generally adopted by the photographic fraternity.

2d. BOWDISH'S POLISHING PRESS FOR PHOTOGRAPHS.

3d. BOWDISH'S PATENT BALANCED CAMERA STAND,

N. S. Bowdish, Patentee.

4th. COLE & BOWDISH'S PATENT BALANCED REVERSIBLE VALVE,

For Steam Engines.

ROBERTS' EUREKA GIANT,

A NEW Hydraulic Motor, invented in 1872, by N. C. Roberts, now of Leonardsville, Madison Co., N. Y. This popular *Water Wheel* is rapidly coming into general use.

10*

CONCLUSION.

We have gleaned as best we could the foregoing history, for the use of the present and future inhabitants of this place, and the strangers within our gates. We have endeavored to arrange the facts in an attractive and interesting form, embellished by the creations of fancy only to the extent justified by the subject. We do not expect that many will experience the same interest and pleasure in its perusal that we have in its compilation. As a national characteristic, we are too intensely occupied with the present, to give much attention or thought to the past; and yet, in our more serious moments, and especially when age turns our thoughts and affections inward and backward, we love to look for the landmarks of bygone years.

Beyond the French War, all in the history of this region is firmly locked in the dark, mysterious past.

The Pyramids of Egypt, it is supposed, were built more than 5,500 years ago, but not a trace of the subsequent history of their builders can be found, except as read in those stupendous artificial relics. Silent and grand in the midst of the ruins of 5,000 years, they stand, to astonish and amaze the world.

But no green thing grows there now. All is ruin and desolation. Not so with Nature's grand monuments around Richfield. Of far more ancient date, they can boast a supreme Architect and Builder, who still lives, and his invisible agencies never cease to give fresh touches of beauty to these sublime works, making them "*a joy forever.*" It required no centuries of the unpaid toil of millions of vassals to erect these beautiful hills, these continuous mountains—to hollow out these lakes, and fit them to receive and garner the springs, rivulets, and brooks flowing into their bosom. Nor was earth's great Chemist indifferent to the attractions of this natural amphitheatre. Alas! that the mountains should waste their centuries in looking down in solemn silence upon the lonely valley. It shall not be. From earth's hidden laboratory the waters gush forth. A crowd is gathered around this modern Bethesda; all may come and be healed. Unlike the ancient pool, no waiting is required, for the healing angel gives it his constant attention— none are sent empty away. The benefits derived from the use of these waters, by thousands now living, assure the future of Richfield. Its location, surroundings, and the diversity and efficacy of its mineral waters, place it beyond the competition of any watering-place now popularly known. To very many of its early patrons it has become a second home, and the return of their happy faces on the opening of the seasons is looked for as a matter of course.

By others it is sought as a *dernier ressort* for the relief of ills that other means have failed to secure. We can therefore confidently commit the future of the place to coming generations, believing the sons of such heroic sires will not fail to nobly emulate them in all commendable public enterprises and private virtues.

THE END.